Forged by Love

by

Laura Strickland

The Lobster Cove Series

Forged by Love

Cover Art by *Diana Carlile*

The Wild Rose Press, Inc.
PO Box 708
Adams Basin, NY 14410-0708
Visit us at www.thewildrosepress.com

Publishing History
First American Rose Edition, 2015
Print ISBN 978-1-5092-0637-7
Digital ISBN 978-1-5092-0458-8

The Lobster Cove Series
Published in the United States of America

Josie stared at the man who spoke, afraid to believe her eyes. Tall and with bare shoulders that gleamed in the sun, he had a crop of wavy black hair and skin almost as dark as her own. Though he spoke to Daniel, his brown eyes sought hers and held them, his wonder evident to see.

Not remember him? From the instant he stepped on the wharf, Josie's attention had been snagged—and not just because he was a good-looking man. No, for the pull she'd felt from the first they sighted this place heightened almost unbearably, every one of her inner instincts sitting up and howling.

Not remember him? Had there been a moment since that night he hadn't been, somehow, with her?

Her lips parted, but she didn't speak. Daniel's deep voice sounded instead.

"Of course, of course we remember you, sir. How could we forget?"

"Good to see you again." The man focused on Daniel at last and extended a hand to him without hesitation. "But what sort of happenstance has brought you here where we might cross paths again?"

"A long story, sir, and one with a full measure of sorrow." Daniel shook the man's hand with the innate courtesy that always marked him.

The fellow's gaze stole back to Josie, and she promptly went breathless. "I'm very glad to see you safe. That night—well, I never did get your names."

"Daniel Freeman, sir. This here is my son Michael, his wife Eunice, and their child Hetty. And my own girl, Josie."

Praise for Laura Strickland

"The world building is phenomenal."
~*Daysie W. at My Book Addiction and More*
~*~

"Laura Strickland creates a world that not only draws you in, but she incorporates it…seamlessly. …the kind of book that keeps you awake well into the wee hours, and sighing with satisfaction when you've finished the very last page."
~*Nicole McCaffrey, author*
~*~

"As I read I became so involved with the story, I found it difficult to put down the book. …Definitely …an author to watch."
~*Dandelion at Long & Short Reviews*

Books by Laura Strickland
available from The Wild Rose Press, Inc.
Dead Handsome: A Buffalo Steampunk Adventure
Off Kilter: A Buffalo Steampunk Adventure
Devil Black
His Wicked Highland Ways
Daughter of Sherwood
Champion of Sherwood
Lord of Sherwood
The White Gull
Forged by Love
Honor Bound: A Highland Adventure
~*~

Christmas Stories:
Mrs. Claus and the Viking Ship
The Tenth Suitor

Chapter One

Lobster Cove, Maine, August 1865

Douglas Grier flipped the glowing bar of orange-hot metal over on the anvil and struck it a measured blow. Sweat trickled freely down his naked back, prompted by a combination of heat and effort. The door of the forge stood open to the afternoon—bright and sunny after last night's storm—but nary a breath of breeze stirred.

He scrutinized the metal, destined to become part of a spar on a lobster trawler, and pumped up the fire without conscious thought. When he'd been away fighting in the south, attached to the second Maine regiment, he'd longed for just this—long days of hard work, the skill and labor of coaxing the metal to his will, the comfort of this place that so often seemed the closest he'd ever known to a real home.

Who'd think that, back at last, he would have such a hard time adjusting?

War changed a man. He'd heard that over and over again since he returned—sometimes spoken to his face in philosophical tones by men who hadn't been there, sometimes whispered and accompanied by sidelong glances. He supposed anything repeated that often must be true.

He grunted and flipped the bar again. He felt rather

than saw his boss, Rab Sinclair, shoot him an inquiring look. Rab frequently kept an affectionate eye on him, one of the things Douglas had missed most while he was away. But Rab, standing with his brawny arms crossed and talking to a customer, didn't pause in his conversation.

To be sure, the shop seemed uncommonly crowded this afternoon. No fewer than five customers had made their way in, and Rab's children were underfoot as well, the two youngest ducking and playing tag as they so often did. Douglas couldn't count the times their ma had scolded them for that. And the eldest, Dorothea, sat on the top of a workbench swinging her feet and talking for all she was worth to Douglas's former teacher, Mrs. Applegate.

Douglas stole a look at her and smiled to himself, his mood instantly improving. No one could stay gloomy in Dorothea Sinclair's company. Douglas would warrant she'd make the Devil himself grin in delight.

If Douglas had a little sister—he didn't, he had a younger brother instead, only a year or so older than Dora—he'd want her to be just like Dorothea Sinclair, bright as a brass button and twice as pretty, with black hair like her father's, and her mother's dreamy eyes.

He cocked his ear now and picked up her conversation.

"I'm determined for it, Mrs. Applegate. I've been saving all my egg money, and as soon as I have enough, I'll send off to Augusta for that writing course. I mean to be the very next Louisa May Alcott."

Her listener smiled. Mrs. Applegate had been called Miss Cooper before she married the new town lawyer and went to having babies. She still mentored Dorothea, much as Rab Sinclair had him, Douglas. In fact, it had been Mrs. Applegate who'd talked Rab into apprenticing Douglas fourteen years ago, when he was nothing but a skinny, fatherless tadpole.

Fatherless, still.

He straightened and lowered the weighted hammer to look around the familiar, dearly loved place.

The scene seemed to waver before his eyes and, as it had lately, memory intruded: a far different setting and images much less welcome.

Blood and mud, an endless sea of both. The screams of wounded horses—a sound Douglas would never forget—the cries of men strapped down beneath the surgeon's saw. The seemingly endless *boom, boom, boom* of cannon that rattled his teeth and got inside him, shook his innards till he wanted to throw up.

He'd been fortunate though, he told himself firmly. *Fortunate*. The Union Army had been quick to make use of his skill at the forge, attaching him to an encampment just behind their lines. He didn't have to wear the blue uniform that strained over his burly shoulders—at least not all the time—nor carry the rifle with its deadly bayonet, which had surely been invented by the Devil himself.

He had been called upon to use his skills for a variety of causes, from mending caissons on the fly to cauterizing the stumps of severed limbs. There had even been that one time…

He drew a breath that expanded his broad chest, remembering, and the forge disappeared before his eyes. Instead he saw a dark night and a white moon, sharp and cruel as a sickle, flying before a hot wind.

Douglas had been roused from his weary bed by his friend, Donner, who worked supply for their outfit and had his fingers in a host of pies.

"Shh!" Donner cautioned him at once. "Don't wake anybody up."

That had been enough to make Douglas swallow the curse that hovered on his lips. Only half dressed, he rose from the narrow cot and followed Donner out into the gusty darkness.

"Fetch your pincers, hammer, or whatever else you'll need to break iron," Donner whispered. "I got a job for you."

The army had fitted out a mobile forge for Douglas that could move along with their lines. He ducked inside and snatched the required tools without looking. "What—?" he began.

"Shush," Donner said again. "Nobody can know."

Without further explanation, Donner led him off through a cornfield, half of which had been burned in the wake of the retreating Confederate army. Nearly a year before the end of the war this had been, somewhere in southern Virginia. Douglas remembered the scent of the stalks surrounding him as he struggled to push through them following the much smaller Donner. On the far side of the field stood a copse of trees, and there, close beneath their shelter, had gathered a group of people—two Union soldiers, neither of whom Douglas recognized, and five Negroes huddled close together as if they shared one heart.

Startled, he shot a look at Donner. They had strict orders to steer clear of the local populace, brown or white, and not involve themselves in what their corporal called "politics."

"You're here to fight." *Maim, mutilate, and slaughter people.* Right, and what had that to do with politics?

"What—" he began again.

In a low voice, Donner replied. "They're on the run. We're helping them."

"Escaping?" Douglas could not tell which appalled him more, the idea that one man might honestly suppose he owned another or being dragged from his cot to become enmeshed in such a situation.

No one said anything, and Douglas tumbled to the foolishness of his question. What else would they be doing out here behind the northern lines in the middle of the night?

One of the Union soldiers spoke after a lengthy pause. To his further surprise, Douglas caught the glint of sergeant's stripes on his sleeve.

"Their plantation about five miles west of here burned—house, slave quarters, and all. They made it away in the confusion. Crosby, here, is going to smuggle them back farther behind the lines and away."

Douglas nodded, realizing not all the stench of burning came from the field.

"Men after us," said one of the Negroes, his voice deep as the night. "Don't have much time."

Douglas eyed the group of two men and three women. In the light from the moon their faces had a similarity born of expression, all stoic caution. The man who had spoken had grizzled hair, and the second, who looked younger, might have been his son. One woman, clearly elderly, wore a kerchief knotted around her head and leaned on a stick; the other two appeared much younger.

"They're chained up," Donner explained. "Need you to break them apart."

Chained?

The older man raised fisted hands, and Douglas saw it for truth. Emotion tore through him; he didn't lose his temper often, but it wasn't every day he saw people constrained like livestock.

He gave a hard nod and gestured the fellow forward to a boulder that lay at the edge of the field. "I'll be glad to."

The man moved, and the others came with him. Only then did Douglas see they were not only each shackled but chained to one another, as well.

Grimly, and choking back hard on his outrage, he set to work. All dignity, the old fellow bent and laid his hands across the rock; Douglas carefully placed his chisel and raised the hammer to force the hasp. The sharp sound of breaking metal seemed to echo through the night.

The younger man shouldered the elder aside eagerly and laid his clenched fists on the rock. Moving quickly now, Douglas transferred his anger into force that made short work of the man's shackles, which the fellow then kicked aside before he helped one of the younger women to his place.

When she bent down, Douglas saw she was heavy with child. She, in turn, assisted the old woman; Douglas worked gently on those fetters and moved them away carefully when they came off.

The last of the women quickly stooped to hunker at his feet. She stretched her hands eagerly across the cold rock, and Douglas glanced up to encounter her face, lit by the moonlight.

She was beautiful. Young and willowy, with a smooth brow, prominent cheekbones, and a tapered chin, she had hair that crinkled all around her face and great, wide eyes even darker than Douglas's own. For an instant their gazes connected, and it felt just as if someone punched Douglas in the heart. For surely he could glimpse her soul in those eyes—twice as beautiful as her face.

"Hurry," Donner bade.

She had delicate wrists and slender, clenched fingers that made the shackles seem an even greater abomination. With all his heart Douglas wanted the cruel, dirty, rusted metal away from her skin. He accomplished the task with a series of sharp blows, and when the chains fell away she grasped his hands.

"Thank you. Thank you, sir!"

And what a voice she had! Deep for a woman's, and soft as velvet. Douglas stood like a man struck—or stupid—while she scrambled up and, with a lingering look for him, joined her companions.

Donner laid a hand on Douglas's shoulder. "Best night's work you ever did, I'll bet."

Douglas nodded, giving it but half his attention, too busy regretting the loss of the young woman's touch.

The sergeant gathered his little flock. Another of the soldiers snatched up the broken shackles and chains. A hot wind stirred the branches, and a cloud moved across the moon, sending flickering light into Douglas's eyes. Yet he saw how she looked back at him still, her gaze once more reaching for his.

Laughter in the forge brought him back to himself and the scene—one he had already relived a hundred times—disappeared from his mind's eye.

7

He had no regrets about the task he'd performed that night, save one: he should have asked her name. Why had he failed to ask her name so he might hold it in his heart?

Chapter Two

Josie Freeman stood at the rail of the *Intrepid* and eyed the coastline toward which the ship struggled. Well-forested, rugged and green, to her eyes it looked like the back of beyond, or maybe the ends of the earth. She knew it couldn't be the end, though. They were meant to sail on still farther northward, if only the captain and crew could get the ship set right.

At the thought, her stomach roiled within her once more. She stood at the rail for a reason—no fit sailor, she. The sickness had barely left her alone since they'd embarked at Philadelphia, and last night's storm had about finished her.

Northward, northward…the word repeated in her head like a magical charm as it had for so long. Ever since that terrible night they'd left the plantation with fear on their backs, running through fields, hiding in barns and the occasional safe house until eventually making their way to Philadelphia.

Josie lifted her chin in an unconscious gesture of resolve. They had lost—and gained—so much along the way. Rainie had died on the trail somewhere south of Pennsylvania, taking a big piece of Josie's heart with her.

She blinked away tears even now, remembering. With bloodhounds on their trail, they'd barely paused long enough to bury the old woman who'd been like a grandmother to Josie.

But, she reminded herself, they'd gained their freedom, purchased by Rainie and so many others.

She gazed across the deck of the ship at her father, who stood speaking with the captain. Well, then, Daniel Freeman was not in truth her father—just her mother's husband. He'd taken the name "Freeman" on all their behalf when they reached Pennsylvania, putting that other, hated name behind them.

Daniel it was who'd kept them strong, even as Rainie had given them heart. Josie's brother, Michael, lent them determination with his unflinching will to live free; his wife, Eunice, and their child, Hetty, gave Josie the only sense of family she could claim.

Still together, the five of them were now indeed destined for the unknown—a former slave settlement in another world called Nova Scotia that lay beyond Josie's imagining. In a foreign country, it was, and Mrs. Hobbs from the Society of Friends back in Philadelphia, who had helped them for so long, claimed they would at last be beyond the reach of the hate that dogged them.

Josie shivered in the hot, humid air. She didn't believe that yet—dared not—for she could feel hate right here aboard ship with them. It sounded in the whispers of the crew, showed in their sidelong glances and the talk she'd overheard about bad luck and curses. Some of the sailors thought it was courting misfortune to have them aboard, even claimed a hex had summoned up last night's storm that left the *Intrepid* damaged and limping.

Daniel crossed the deck to Josie's side. His intelligent gaze inspected her kindly before he said,

"How you feeling, child? Better?"

Josie shook her head. "We need to get off this ship. I can feel the ill will."

Daniel didn't argue it; he respected Josie's instincts and intuition, understood that when she *felt* things they all too often proved true.

"Captain says we can put in at a town just ahead. Claims it's a quiet place where nobody will get wind of us. Once the ship's repaired, we'll sail on to the Weaver Settlement."

But Josie didn't want to sail on; everything inside her railed against it. "And what's there for us, do you know?"

Daniel shrugged and put his arm around her. "Freedom, I hope. A new life."

Freedom and hope. Both seemed so very distant. Josie closed her eyes and leaned into Daniel's quiet strength.

"I'm tired, Daniel. And sick. Not so sure I can go on." She would have been happy staying in Philadelphia—or, if not happy, at least content. She'd had a job there and had even started making friends among others of the freed community. No sooner had she begun to feel secure, though, than word came— Massa Collingwood had sent men after them, paid men. Slave hunters.

But, she'd protested when they told her, she and her family were no longer slaves. Supposedly they'd been emancipated. Of course that was just on paper, and in her heart Josie knew it for untruth. They were slaves so long as their former owner considered them his property, in defiance of the law—and sent men to hunt down and recapture them.

Folk still got recaptured every day. Josie had heard the harrowing stories of men dragged away from new wives, women torn from their children's arms and smuggled off in the night, never to be seen again.

Josie swallowed a gout of sickness. She knew Buford Collingwood, knew that if he'd sent men after them it was out of combined arrogance and spite.

Hadn't he sold Josie's ma away for the same reasons?

The *Intrepid* lurched as the crew struggled to bring her round to the land. Daniel steadied Josie against his shoulder. The green, forested shore—all rock and high bluffs—suddenly opened up like a lover reaching his arms to invite Josie in.

She saw a sheltered harbor with a long, wooden dock and a number of boats at anchor. Beyond it climbed the land and what must be this town Daniel mentioned, a series of dirt roads and houses. Josie's wondering eyes even picked out the spire of a church.

She blinked. A pretty enough place, but would she be safe here?

No sooner had the question entered her mind than the clouds split overhead, the last of the night's storm blowing away. Sunlight streamed down in ladders to kiss the town.

Daniel's deep chuckle sounded in Josie's ear. "There now, girl. You're always going on about signs and portents. How's that for an omen?"

"Good," Josie had to admit.

His arm tightened around her. "Josie, honey, you know I love you like a daughter, don't you?"

"Oh, yes, Daniel."

"We've trod a hard path so far. But believe me

when I tell you there's better ahead—just like that sun coming through those clouds. You remember that, when you start feeling afraid, hear?"

Josie gazed into the old man's face, and her heart swelled. Daniel might not be her father in truth, but as far back as she could remember he had always been there with his big, warm hands and his boundless kindness. A girl couldn't ask for better.

And yes, she had to remember the blessings scattered in among all the hurts—had to keep looking for them, those little miracles that made it possible to go on.

Only some miracles—like Daniel—weren't so small.

She scanned the rocky harbor again. Did this place hold anything for her? How could it? But if not, then why did she feel such a powerful pull toward it?

The captain, with his neat blue uniform and serious eyes, joined them at the rail.

"Sorry for the delay, folks. We'll put in here and see what repairs are needed, get the ship mended as soon as we can, and be back underway. I know the rudder's damaged, along with that mast. Hope there's not much more."

"Thank you, Captain Roberts. Will we be able to find lodging here?"

"I hope so, Mr. Freeman. Lobster Cove's a small town, but often folks have rooms to let."

Daniel nodded, but Josie could feel his doubt. Uncertainty ahead and the hounds following behind—it seemed not so much had changed since Virginia, after all.

Chapter Three

Douglas and Rab Sinclair worked in tandem—as they did so often—to shoe Andrew Deacon's big draft horse, Douglas beating the new shoes into shape and Rab grappling with the animal, his great shoulder muscles bunching as he stood bent with one saucer-sized hoof steadied between his knees.

Most of the customers had gone and, with the children chased off to the house Rab had built up the shore, peace had descended. Only Mr. Deacon stood by, and him a man of few words.

Douglas watched Rab's black hair tumble over his brow, seeing for the first time that it now contained a few threads of silver. Had those been there before Douglas went away to war? He couldn't say, but his heart clenched within him. Of all the things that might change in his world, he wanted this least—wished that Rab Sinclair should never age, nor his lovely little wife, Lisbeth. Douglas didn't even want to imagine his life without them in it.

He and Rab worked so well together, after all these years, they barely needed words. Lisbeth often teased that they were like bears who communicated in grunts. Douglas smiled to himself and admitted she might not be far wrong.

But it felt so comfortable being with someone who neither gave orders nor needed directions.

Though little more than ten years separated them in age, Rab Sinclair represented the only father Douglas could claim. From Rab he'd learned to work hard, to keep his word, and be patient with those he cared about—in short, to be a man. Even before Douglas's mother, Maggie, took up with a traveler and left, back when Douglas was sixteen—taking Douglas's younger brother, Timmy, but leaving Douglas behind—he'd found solace in being here amid the clang of metal and beside the steadily burning fire.

He'd just finished beating the fourth shoe into shape when Billy Dixon's grandson, Bart, burst in through the door of the forge, all excitement.

"Mr. Sinclair, my grandpa says you hafta come! There's a foundered ship in the harbor, and they need your help."

Rab tipped his head up, sweat glistening on his brow. "Urgent is it, lad? Only you can see I am in the middle of something."

"They say they need a blacksmith for the repairs."

Rab glanced at Douglas. "You go, Dougie. I can finish this."

Douglas nodded. Rab, the only person in his world who still addressed him using the diminutive, pronounced it "Doogie," the Scots burr coloring his deep voice despite all his years away from his homeland.

Bart fixed Douglas with an excited gaze. "Come quick, they said."

Douglas went as he stood—half dressed in just trousers and his leather apron, the sweat still standing out on him.

Outside, he saw the day had grown late; most folks

had probably gone home to supper. Or maybe they had moved to the harbor, which he saw was thronged with people as he and Bart arrived.

He stared with some interest at the newly arrived vessel. Deep-water ships didn't often make it into Lobster Cove, though the harbor could accommodate them if necessary. Even to his eye this one looked heavily damaged, listing slightly to one side and with a broken mast. A victim of last night's blow, no doubt.

And that explained all the people at the harbor—the ship must have been carrying passengers as well as cargo.

From among the many, Douglas picked out Billy Dixon standing with a group of fishermen, sailors, and another fellow who could only be the captain of the damaged vessel.

Ignoring everyone else, Douglas jogged over to them. Two of the men in the group he knew for boat builders—apparently called in to help the crew with repairs.

"Here he is now," said Billy Dixon when Douglas reached them, and the ship's captain turned shrewd eyes on him.

Douglas, who didn't often waste words, nodded, and Billy launched into an explanation of the situation.

"Captain Roberts, here, would like to get back underway as soon as he might. He's got passengers to consider, see. We think we can get that broken mast replaced, though we've never done one that size. But the rudder's gone, as well, snapped like kindling."

One of the sailors touched Douglas on the arm. "Here, look at this."

They had disassembled what could only be part—

or all—of the ship's rudder and spread the pieces on the wharf. Well-seasoned oak that showed breaks running through the grain like fresh wounds had been lined up with iron rods now slick with salt water and rust. Douglas ran a quick eye over them, tracing what should be an assembly.

Billy asked him, "You think you and Rab could knock up something to replace those broken pieces? This one's sheered right off, and the others are 'bout ready to go."

Douglas hunkered down on the dock to get a closer look. "Might take some doing, and some time."

"How long?" the captain inquired. "I have folks need to get up to Nova Scotia as soon as possible."

"Well, sir, they may have to wait a few days." Douglas straightened and looked the man in the eye. "That mast won't get fixed easy, either. You may be able to find your passengers lodging here in town. Some folks will let a room in their house, for the coin."

"I can only hope so, but as befits some of my passengers, I confess, I have my doubts." The captain directed a significant look toward a little knot of people who stood just along the wharf, not thirty paces away.

Douglas followed his gaze and froze in shock. The group consisted of two men and two women, one with a child in arms, and all Negroes.

A queer rush of emotion arose inside him, and the sun seemed to flicker before his eyes, turned moonlight and shadow—and the scent of burning.

He knew them—surely he did.

All wore respectable, dark-colored clothing far too unexceptional to account for the attention they were being given. The elder of the two men had a bare head

17

that shone grizzled in the sunlight; the younger, who stood with his arm around the woman with the child, wore a cloth cap. They had a pitifully small collection of belongings gathered around their feet.

But Douglas disregarded all that. The second woman…

Across the wharf he made eye contact with her, and his heart stuttered in his chest. It couldn't be. Not here, in Lobster Cove. Because coincidences like that just didn't happen.

Yet he had no doubt, only pure certainty that flooded him like gladness. Like relief.

With a muttered, "Excuse me," he moved along the wharf, precisely as if drawn by chains.

****

"Hello, folks. Sir, I don't suppose you remember me."

Josie stared at the man who spoke, afraid to believe her eyes. Tall and with bare shoulders that gleamed in the sun, he had a crop of wavy black hair and skin almost as dark as her own. Though he spoke to Daniel, his brown eyes sought hers and held them, his wonder evident to see.

Not remember him? From the instant he stepped on the wharf, Josie's attention had been snagged—and not just because he was a good-looking man. No, for the pull she'd felt from the first they sighted this place heightened almost unbearably, every one of her inner instincts sitting up and howling.

Not remember him? Had there been a moment since that night he hadn't been, somehow, with her?

Her lips parted, but she didn't speak. Daniel's deep voice sounded instead.

"Of course, of course we remember you, sir. How could we forget?"

"Good to see you again." The man focused on Daniel at last and extended a hand to him without hesitation. "But what sort of happenstance has brought you here where we might cross paths again?"

"A long story, sir, and one with a full measure of sorrow." Daniel shook the man's hand with the innate courtesy that always marked him.

The fellow's gaze stole back to Josie, and she promptly went breathless. "I'm very glad to see you safe. That night—well, I never did get your names."

"Daniel Freeman, sir. This here is my son Michael, his wife Eunice, and their child Hetty. And my own girl, Josie."

"Douglas Grier, and I'm glad to meet you properly."

Michael leaned forward to shake Douglas Grier's hand. "I'm happy, Mr. Grier, to have a chance to thank you. It was a fine thing you did for us that night."

Douglas Grier smiled, and his somber face transformed as if lit from within. Josie's heart fluttered like a wild bird before resuming a double-time beat.

Calm yourself, girl. He's done no more than look at you.

Grier turned to her. "Josie Freeman," he repeated as if he memorized it, and took Josie's hand.

She promptly went dizzy as sudden images pressed upon her, blotting out the present. His hands coming at her, so strong and yet gentle, out of the darkness that night. The way he'd touched her, with such care and respect, and the way he'd looked at her as if he could see right down to the bottom of her soul.

He smiled again and Josie's poor heart pounded in response. "What a marvel this is. I've wondered a hundred times what happened to you after that night."

He released her hand and glanced around. "But there was another, an older lady."

"Rainie didn't make it, sir," Michael replied evenly, letting none of his grief show. The old woman's death had been a terrible blow to all of them. "She went down one night not long after we met you—chased by hounds."

"God!" Some of the dusky color drained from Douglas Grier's cheek. "I'm so sorry."

A single tear trickled down Eunice's face. "She's an angel now, Mr. Grier, and she left her strength with us."

He nodded, dark hair gleaming in the sun. "I've been called down to help with repairs to the ship." Directing his gaze to Daniel, he went on, "Mr. Freeman, sir, I hope you'll let me assist you during your stay. I need to finish up here, but after that I'd be happy to take you around town and see about finding lodging."

Daniel turned his head and surveyed the town, not revealing his emotions, but Josie knew he wondered what sort of reception they would receive in this far northern place.

"Well, sir," he said slowly, "I'd be obliged."

Douglas smiled again, catching Josie in the edges of the radiance. "I won't be long," he promised. "Wait for me."

Chapter Four

The bright sunlight had begun to fade before Douglas returned to the little family gathered on the wharf. Several others of the passengers had already made their way up into town; the Freemans had merely pulled their boxes to the side and seated the women on them while the men stood by.

When Douglas approached, he heard the child crying in a thin wail. They would all be tired and hungry, no doubt feeling like they'd washed up on a strange shore.

All the time he consulted with the men about repairs he'd bounced the problem of where to house the Freemans around in his mind. Lobster Cove had no hotel proper, just a few folks who let rooms from time to time. He figured Mrs. Taylor made the best bet. A widow, she had more space than most.

"Sorry that took so long," he greeted Mr. Freeman. "Didn't like to keep you folks waiting."

Freeman returned, "Don't suppose it can be helped, sir. Any idea how long before that ship can sail?"

"It will be several days, at best."

The family exchanged dismayed glances.

"But if you'll come with me, I'll help find you a place to stay."

Daniel Freeman considered his family with wise eyes. "Baby's ailing. The sea journey didn't go easy with any of us. Michael, you and Eunice stay here. Mr. Grier, Josie and I will come along of you."

Douglas looked at Josie and his heart rose like a gull. *Josie Freeman.* The name suited her and seemed to slip into an empty place in his mind that had waited for it all too long.

Funny how clearly he remembered her from that night even though he'd had only a glimpse of her, how he'd managed in those few moments to measure her height—just up to his ear—and her slender, willowy form, the delicacy of the bones at her wrist, shoulder, and jaw, and those incredible eyes, fringed with long lashes, that dominated her face.

To Daniel he said, "All right, then. We'll try Mrs. Taylor first off. Best leave your luggage for now—we can collect it soon as we secure the place."

Freeman and his daughter followed him from the wharf. They could still hear the child wailing, behind.

Douglas asked as they went, "Why are you folks headed for Nova Scotia? Captain back there said it's where you're bound."

Daniel gave him a tight smile. "Well, sir, things got a mite warm for us back in Philadelphia. Some friends there thought it might be time for us to move on. And there's a community of other folks like us already there, at a place called Weaver Settlement, and thriving— freed slaves."

Douglas glanced at Josie again. "Well, whatever's brought you, it's a right marvel, us crossing paths this way once more."

Daniel answered, "Maybe so. We surely do appreciate your help, sir, more than I can say."

Mrs. Taylor's house stood on Oak, a weathered

saltbox with a neat front garden. To Douglas's surprise, Mrs. Taylor—a diminutive woman wearing a snow-white apron—greeted them at her door, arms crossed over her thin chest. She raked the Freemans with hard eyes before she said, "You needn't bother to ask, Douglas Grier. All my rooms are taken."

Douglas paused in dismay. To be sure, his delay on the wharf must have allowed the other passengers to get ahead of them.

"I'll try Mrs. Blake, shall I?" he asked.

Mrs. Taylor sniffed, went inside, and shut her door.

The hair on the back of Douglas's neck stood up. No stranger to unjust treatment, he. He'd encountered it all his life as a half-breed and son of the town trollop. But now his protective instincts rose, and he burned with embarrassment on the Freemans' behalf. Trying not to reveal the extent of his annoyance, he led them on.

At the next place, they were also told the rooms were all taken, if with less hostility. Douglas didn't know whether to believe Mrs. Blake or not. At the Remingtons, no one consented to answer his knock at the door; he had quickly run out of options.

He paused on Pine with his two charges and took a look around. A barrier of space seemed to enclose the three of them just as if they carried a sickness that kept others away. Even as he stood looking he saw a couple cross the road to detour around them.

He looked at Josie and ached on her behalf, thought about the tired couple and wailing child back on the wharf.

"I'm so sorry," he said. "I can't understand it, but all the rooms seem to be…taken."

"Not your fault, sir," Daniel said with quiet dignity. "Just the way it is. Maybe the captain will let us bunk aboard the ship."

Douglas caught a flash of dismay in Josie's eyes, quickly suppressed. He made a swift decision. "No need for that. I know a place you can stay."

"Eh?"

"Come along. We'll get Miss Freeman, here, settled and then go back for the rest of your family."

What would Rab say when Douglas turned up with five houseguests? He might not know; the forge might well be shut by now. And Rab had given Douglas the snug quarters in back of the shop years ago, after Douglas's mother moved away and abandoned him. The Sinclairs had run out of room by then and were already living in the new place just outside town.

He led Freeman and Josie round back, as the shop did indeed stand quiet, and took them inside.

"Sorry for the mess." No housekeeper, he; the cramped interior screamed bachelor quarters. Dirty dishes lay in the basin beside the cold hearth, and his clothes were scattered across the bed. "And sorry the place is so small. You'll all have to fit yourselves into this one room, I'm afraid. But it's tight and snug."

Josie glanced around. "Who lives here?"

Douglas did not answer. "There's a pump just outside the door. And the wee housie's at the back of the yard." Meeting Freeman's inquiring look he explained, "That's what my boss, Mr. Sinclair, calls it, being that he's from Scotland."

Daniel shook his head. "These your quarters, sir?"

"Doesn't matter whose place it is. It's available, and your family needs a place to stay. You say the baby's ill? Nothing serious, I hope."

Josie answered, "Hetty doesn't like the water." She smiled and pressed her hands to her stomach. "Just like me. You're a kind man, Mr. Grier."

"That's the truth, and we'll accept since it's only for a day or two," Daniel said, stiff with pride. "But we'll pay the owner some rent."

"He'll be insulted if you try. All these months wondering what happened to you folks—I'm just grateful you're here. Like I said, it's a right miracle."

"A right miracle," Josie repeated.

****

Daniel accompanied Douglas Grier back to the harbor to fetch the rest of the family and their belongings.

Josie, her legs finally failing her, sank onto a stool. Her head spun slowly, and she wished she could reach out, grasp hold of her world, and drag it to a halt. It had happened a lot lately, this feeling of disorientation and the desperate need to bring some normalcy to her existence.

Ever since last night's storm, since she'd been told they had to put ashore and she began to feel that powerful pull inside, nothing had been close to ordinary.

She closed her eyes and unfurled her inner sense, which now proved so insistent. No question but the pull came from that man, Douglas Grier.

Lord, how handsome he was. But that had little to do with the situation. He was kind, as well. She had no doubt he'd given them his own place to sleep. His very spirit lingered here, the faint scent of him mingled with those of ash and hot metal from what must be the forge, beyond.

She opened her eyes, got to her feet, and tiptoed to the curtain that screened the doorway opposite. Peeking through, she saw the place lay dim and quiet, the fire well-banked, warmth hovering like a benevolent cloud.

Josie drew a breath. She'd stepped into his world. Who said prayers weren't answered?

Even though she'd begun to doubt it. True, fate had blessed her in many ways: she'd been born to a house slave and raised in the big plantation house, companion to Massa Collingwood's own daughter Alice. Accordingly, she'd learned some skills that would serve her well in years to come. And yes, the fire had come just when Massa Collingwood cast Eunice off for being too heavy with child and turned his eyes in Josie's direction.

She'd prayed about that, right enough. But not nearly so hard as she'd prayed against all odds to see the young blacksmith with the strong hands and respectful eyes again.

Against all odds.

Yet here she stood. She turned her back on the drowsing forge and, without actual intent, began to tidy the room. She folded Douglas Grier's clothes and laid them on the foot of the bed, giving in to impulse and pressing one garment—a soft shirt—to her nose first. Eyes closed once more, she inhaled his scent, and her heart stirred powerfully within her. She continued around the room, setting things to rights and gathering up dirty dishes.

He obviously lived alone. She shouldn't glory in that but found she did. She put all the dishes in the wash basin and went out back to fetch water.

Dark had almost come. Moths and other night insects flitted around the yard, and the first stars poked out overhead. Josie tipped her face to the sky and whispered, "Well, Rainie, what do you think? Am I meant to be here?" One of the stars winked, and Josie answered, "I think so too."

****

By the time Daniel and Douglas Grier came back with the others, Josie had a fire burning and the dishes clean. Douglas ushered in Michael, Eunice, and little Hetty now fast asleep in Michael's arms, and carried in the boxes and bags, shooting a startled look around the place as he did.

The space was indeed tight for five, but comfortable. Josie, grateful the floor didn't rock beneath her feet, helped stow most of their belongings along one wall while Eunice settled Hetty on the bed.

Douglas Grier then moved to the shelves beside the hearth. "Food enough here for you to fix a meal, folks. Use whatever you need and make yourselves comfortable as you can. I'll grab a few things, some clothes and a blanket, and get out of your way. Just so you know, the forge gets going pretty early. If you hear somebody moving around in the shop out there, it will be either me or my boss, Rab Sinclair. Hope we won't disturb you too much."

"Never mind that." Michael stepped up and once more offered Douglas his hand. "This place is a God's send, Mr. Grier. We're grateful."

Douglas nodded, looking embarrassed, before going to gather what he would need for the night. Josie wondered where he would go. Out into the soft darkness of this strange, half-wild place, away from her?

But she knew now he couldn't truly leave her; they were connected somehow deep inside. And she had only to close her eyes again to feel the pull of that connection, like a call made and answered.

Thank you, she thought at him as he moved to the door, and he looked right at her, gave a flash of that smile that had the power to curl her toes.

"See you tomorrow," he told her.

Tomorrow. She couldn't recall when she'd looked forward to the next day of her life quite so much.

Chapter Five

Douglas awoke from a dream of fire and darkness, the scent of hot metal in his nostrils. For a moment he couldn't recall where he was—back in the army encampment, sleeping as he so often had under the wagon that transported his mobile forge? Out back of the Hogshead Tavern in the little malodorous house where he'd been raised?

No. He could see the last stars fading from a dawn sky, and the edge of a porch roof beneath which he lay. Slowly, the horror of his dream faded and reality took its place. He lay on the Sinclairs' back porch, where he'd decided to bunk last night.

Sure enough, he could hear voices coming from inside if he listened hard enough—everybody was up ahead of him. He caught the rumble of Rab's bass, and Lisbeth's lighter answers. Footsteps pattered and a door slammed. The two youngest of the family, Archie and Alisdair, set to talking as they usually did, a mile a minute.

Douglas lay still in his blanket nest as the last pieces fell into place.

Josie Freeman.

His heart skipped a beat and then slammed against his ribs as her face danced before his mind's eye. Those great, wide eyes, a delicate little chin and lips made for kissing. She spoke to him without words. But he wanted to take the trouble from her eyes, replace it with a smile, desired it as he could not remember ever wanting anything.

How?

He lay there pondering the question while the house behind him burgeoned with life and the day grew strong around him. A marvel, pure and simple, that he'd seen her again. If not for the storm and the *Intrepid* foundering, it would never have happened. But the *Intrepid* would be repaired—that meant he had only days, at best.

Days to…what? Persuade her to stay here in Lobster Cove, where she couldn't even secure the offer of lodging? To part ways with her family, likely the only people she had in the world?

For what, to stay with *him*?

Yes, yes, yes. Because she belonged with him, she was already part of him, and he couldn't lose her again. He had only to make her see the truth of that.

In a matter of days. Before the ship sailed.

And, his mind ran on, offer her what? A home? Marriage? His life? Yes, all those things.

She'd think him a madman.

Well, and maybe he was. He'd never so much as contemplated marriage before, had intended to remain a bachelor all his life. Now he knew he'd trade every intention and work his whole life long if he could have Josie Freeman at his side.

A door opened close at hand. A moment later, a great black head came pushing into his face and a wet tongue slapped his cheek.

"Chieftain!"

The Sinclairs always had a Newfoundland dog;

Kelpie had been the first and Chieftain was the third, a worthy successor. Having greeted Douglas to his satisfaction, the dog ambled off the porch to do his business.

Douglas looked up and saw Lisbeth Sinclair standing in the doorway.

"Well then, Douglas." She smiled at him. "Would you like some breakfast?"

****

Little Hetty, who woke fitful and restless many times during the night, at last stopped crying shortly before morning, and Josie managed to snatch a bit of sleep. She, Eunice, and Hetty shared Douglas Grier's bed, while Michael and Daniel lay on the floor.

Josie expected more troubled dreams but slept too hard and too deep. She rose at dawn and made up the fire before going out to visit what Douglas had called the "wee hoosie."

Then she stood and watched the new day bleed light across the sky. Where might Douglas be now? What did her inner sense tell her about him?

That he was strong and steady, sure as the rock that underlay this place—a haven in this world of storm, one meant for her.

But how could that be? It made no sense. She from a plantation house in Virginia and he from this far northern place—what could they have in common?

Save feelings.

Yes, well, if Josie had learned one thing in her life, it was that feelings—like people—came and went. The tide of her life never let her hang on to anyone for long.

Her mother, gone. Rainie, gone. Miss Alice, whom Josie had once more than half believed her friend, gone as well. People could disappear in an instant, just like those stars overhead that winked out one by one from the sky.

Why think of Douglas Grier? She would be gone from this town in a few days, the harsh tide pushing her on.

Unless she stayed.

And from whence had come that thought? Crazy, wonderful, terrible thought. He would not ask her, a Negress, to stay. She wouldn't agree if he did.

With a mental shake, she stirred herself and went inside, leaving the pieces of her dreams behind.

****

"Here, let me do that for you."

Josie spun around when the voice sounded behind her, nearly spilling the bucket of water she'd just drawn. Douglas Grier stood at her elbow, as if her thoughts had conjured him. If they had, it had taken all day and a fair bit of conjuring.

She'd seen him from time to time throughout the day, of course. He'd come to greet them when he arrived at the forge that morning, and had introduced them to the owner of the place, Rab Sinclair.

Mr. Sinclair, a big, burly man with kind eyes, had assured them he didn't mind them lodging behind the forge.

"You're most welcome. These are Dougie's quarters anyway, and his to lend as he sees fit."

Doogie. Josie smiled to herself as she tried to apply the name to the man who now stood before her. She liked it.

As if he caught it from her, Douglas smiled also, his somber face transforming in that wonderful way it had.

"You're looking a good bit happier, Miss Freeman."

Josie allowed a hint of mischief to thread her voice. "Maybe I'm just glad to see you, Mr. Grier." She'd never been one to flirt with the men as some of the girls back home did. She'd seen, far too often, where that led. But it seemed to come naturally with this man.

The smile in his eyes deepened. "I hope so. But there's no need for you to call me 'Mr. Grier' or 'sir.' Douglas will do fine between us."

"Or 'Dougie'?" She pronounced it the way Mr. Sinclair did and tipped her head.

"If you like." And what was it vibrated in his deep voice? It seemed to say, call me whatever you wish; just keep speaking to me.

He took the bucket from her hands, and his fingers brushed hers. Just like that, Josie felt a rush. Eunice used to say, back when she first fell in love with Michael—that was before Massa Collingwood took Eunice to his bed—that attraction between men and women was a dance, a pretty thing of stepping backward and forward, the steps known by heart.

Maybe so, because Josie's inexperienced heart sure seemed to know what to do.

Dougie set the pail down carefully and leaned against the back wall of the house. She liked the way he looked in his work clothes as she'd glimpsed him from time to time today, the leather trousers and apron that left his shoulders, back, and part of his chest bare. But now he'd changed into a soft shirt of creamy homespun, the sleeves pushed up over his bronzed forearms.

"Then you'll need to call me 'Josie,' " she told

him.

"*Miss* Josie—I think that fits." Some of the light in his eyes dimmed. "Do you have any idea how many times I thought about you after that night? Wondered what had happened to you, wondered what your name might be. I'm glad to have it, now."

"I thought about you too. What are the chances we'd cross paths this way?"

"Like I said, it truly is a miracle, Miss Josie. You know, I never used to believe in 'em."

"Me neither."

The smile returned to his eyes. He jerked his head toward the doorway. "Full house in there. I'm done for the day and thought you might like a breather. Walk with me? I can show you around town."

"I'd like that." She wiped her palms on her apron and raised her hands to her hair. "Just let me tidy myself—"

"No need. You're beautiful."

His words hung in the darkling yard, an absolute.

He leaned toward her. "So beautiful," he whispered, and Josie's heart took wings. A man of few words, Dougie Grier, but those he did say wove a powerful spell.

They traversed the streets that made up the gridwork of the town—First and Maple, Second and Pine. Dougie pointed out the main buildings, like Sawyer's lumber mill, St. Joseph's Church, and the school he'd once attended. The soft dark settled all around them, and Josie could hear the soft *shush, shush* of the ocean all the way from the harbor.

She barely noticed the looks they received from the few people they passed. All her attention rested on the man beside her, who paced his steps to hers. She clearly felt the tension that gathered within him when he paused in front of a tavern.

"See that little house there, out back?"

Josie barely could, in the gloom. Set off behind the tavern and painted white, it hardly looked like a house at all, smaller even than the quarters behind the forge.

She nodded.

"Where I grew up," he told her. "My ma was barmaid at the Hogshead, there. She—" Abruptly he stopped speaking. Josie felt emotions rush through him, predominantly shame. "She took men back there with her from time to time. One of them must have been my father. Another was my younger brother's father. Best you know that about me, if—"

If? Josie raised questioning eyes to him. If, what? If they were to begin seeing one another, be together? But that was impossible, wasn't it?

"Where is she now, your ma?"

He shrugged. "I don't know. Left here when I was sixteen, ran off with a man. Took my brother."

"And left you?" Even Josie, familiar with no end of cruelties, felt shocked by such pure meanness.

He shrugged again. "Timmy was a lot younger; he needed her more. Besides, she never—never set much store in me."

"She must have been a pure fool, if you'll forgive me saying." Josie pronounced it like fact and reached out to touch his arm. Swiftly, he slid his fingers down until they caught hold of hers.

The rightness of it sounded through Josie like the chime of a bell.

"Come on away from this place," she said. "It

feels—too sad."

"It was sad. Will your father be worrying about where you are?"

"You mean Daniel? He knows where I am—with you."

"Then let me show you a better place."

They went on, hand in hand, through streets now so dark Josie imagined no one would notice. Dougie led her back down Oak to Main, which fronted the harbor. Josie saw the *Intrepid* at rest there, still listing slightly to starboard.

"How long?" Josie asked.

"For what?"

"For the ship to be ready to sail again."

His fingers tightened on hers. "It will be a few days."

Only a few. A new ache pierced Josie's heart, joining the others already there. Could she stand to lose another person from her life?

Yet she'd only just met him.

It doesn't matter, her heart insisted.

They turned north along the shore road, the sea now keeping them company.

"How did you get to working for Mr. Sinclair?" Josie asked then.

"He 'prenticed me when I was thirteen. I believe my teacher, Miss Cooper, talked him into it. I wasn't so sure about it at the start. The work seemed impossible, and I'd never done well at much of anything. I just knew I wanted to spend time there in the shop with him and his dog—that was Kelpie, then. The hero dog."

"Hero?"

"He saved Mrs. Sinclair's life not long after that—

pulled her out of the sea. That was back before she was Mrs. Sinclair."

"Your boss seems a kind man."

"He is, to the bone. Gave me those quarters behind the forge after my ma left and I had nowhere to go. Built his family a house up along here. That's what I want to show you."

They walked a bit farther with the dark gathering all around before he said, "There. See?"

The house stood neat and foursquare, its face to the sea, a white saltbox with a picket fence running all the way around. In front, a garden spilled flowers in profusion. Even as they watched, a light came on in one of the windows.

Softly, Dougie said, "That's the house Rab built for his family, built it with love and his own hands. I helped him a bit, along with Mr. Becker who works at the sawmill, and other folks from town. But it was Rab's gift to Lisbeth, a little bit of heaven."

Josie heard the longing in his voice and understood what it meant. Dougie Grier showed her his past in the tumbledown house behind the tavern, and his hopes for his future, here.

He showed her his dreams.

"There, look." His fingers tightened suddenly on hers. "The first star. Quick, make a wish."

I wish I could stay.

Chapter Six

"Mr. Freeman, I'm happy to tell you the *Intrepid* will be ready to sail tomorrow. Wanted to give you and your family some time to pack up your belongings and get ready. We'll be leaving on the morning tide."

Josie, overhearing Captain Roberts from where he stood at the back door, froze in the act of ladling soup into the bowls on the table. Her heart dropped within her, like a stone.

Five days it had been since she arrived in Lobster Cove—five wonderful days that had passed far too quickly. During that time she'd helped look after this place and tended Hetty and Eunice, but all the while her mind remained centered on the man who worked beyond the curtain, in the forge. It was as if her soul tracked him even when her eyes couldn't.

She'd known this moment must come, carried it like a sickness in the pit of her stomach. She'd even listened for word, hoping to be prepared, but now Captain Roberts slipped up and delivered the blow without warning.

She set the soup pot down carefully and grabbed the edge of the table. Daniel and the captain went on talking, but she no longer heard them. She was too busy thinking back over those five days like a woman reliving a dream.

Life here had so quickly fallen into a pattern. There

were always chores to be done, but regardless, she and Dougie somehow managed to make time for one another. When he finished his work for the day he invariably presented himself at the door like a proper caller and asked her to go walking. They'd thoroughly explored most of the town, and he'd showed her the view from atop the bluffs. He usually brought her some little gift—a flower, or a cake Mrs. Sinclair had baked, and once a four-leaf clover.

He'd tucked that behind her ear, his touch making her shiver like she had a fever.

"For luck," he'd whispered, and she thought for one blinding instant he meant to kiss her. He hadn't kissed her, nor done more than touch her hand—and her ear. A respectful man, was Douglas Grier.

There were times she wished he weren't. Because she ached for his touch, ached to touch him, longed to brush her fingers along those broad shoulders, so often bared when he worked in the forge. To trace the single dimple that appeared in only one cheek when he smiled. To find out how his lips tasted.

Michael and Eunice had begun to look askance when he came to the door. Josie had even heard Michael protest once when she left, and Daniel's response.

"Can't nothing come of it. We'll be leaving soon."

Soon had just become tomorrow morning.

Josie set the ladle beside the pot and, before she could let herself hesitate, slipped through the curtain into the forge.

Mr. Sinclair, working at the anvil, shot her an inquiring look and lifted an eyebrow. "What is it, Miss Freeman?" He took in her expression. "Something wrong?"

"I hoped for a word with Mr. Grier."

Rab smiled. "He's just running a finished job up the street. Why don't you wait out front?"

Josie did, unable to keep still and for once not even noticing the stares of people passing by. Soon enough, Dougie came back, still clad in his work gear. When he saw her, his face lit.

"Miss Josie, you looking for me?"

Desperate, she reached for his hand. "We just had word—we're leaving tomorrow morning."

****

Douglas knew himself to be far less than eloquent. Words rarely came easily to him, and he seldom tried to express what lay in his mind.

This, though, was different. This time Josie Freeman might well be snatched away from him. If ever he attained a degree of eloquence, it had better be now.

He could see and feel her desperation in the way her fingers caught at him, and in her trembling.

Well, but he'd known better than most that repairs to the *Intrepid* were almost complete. He and Rab had furnished the required parts for the rudder assembly, and he'd watched the new mast go into place. That had just left the repairs to the hull, which must have been completed sometime today.

Protest arose in his chest and got a stranglehold on his throat. Somehow he managed to say, "Walk with me."

She came, unquestioning. They'd done a powerful lot of walking together these past days, and sitting together on the rocks above Frenchman Bay, talking.

She'd told him a little about her childhood,

growing up in the big plantation house, so much more fortunate than the children who went to work in the fields at a young age. He gathered, though she didn't really say, she attained that privilege because her ma worked in the house, as well.

Josie had grown up with her owner's daughter, Alice, the two of them nearly inseparable. Sitting through Alice's lessons with her, Josie had learned to read and write, her quick mind making little of the chore. She'd become adept at sewing and embroidery, as well.

Yet she always skipped some details when she spoke, things she would not describe. And when he'd met her, she'd been chained like a hound to others of the house servants. Douglas's mind had trouble making the leap between that and a privileged state of existence. He knew Josie, yet he didn't. Whatever he did or didn't know about her, she fitted him like no one else he'd ever known.

He now had to convince her of that.

They walked down along Main to the harbor and then northward. There, among the rocks, they found their favorite perch. Douglas boosted Josie up and followed her, the silence stretching out like the water at their feet as he flailed inwardly for the right words.

At last, giving it up, he spoke plainly, from his heart. "Don't go."

Her gaze flew to his and held there. Just as it had been that first night when he broke the shackles from her wrists, he felt the connection between them flare.

"Oh, Dougie," she said then, like a woman in mourning. "You tell me how I can stay. How?"

"With me." He ached to take her in his arms,

longed for it so intensely he felt breathless. He wouldn't coerce her. This choice had to be hers.

"My family—" she began.

Of course, her family. All she had in the world. How could he expect her to part with them for *him*?

"They can stay, as well."

Quickly, she shook her head. "This community where we're going—it's full of others like us, former slaves starting over. Aside from that, there's something you don't know. Men are after us—slave-hunters."

"What?"

She made a helpless gesture with her delicate hands. "Massa Collingwood, our master—the man who used to be our master—hired them to bring us back. We found out in Philadelphia. It's why we left."

Douglas turned sick. What sort of man would do such a thing? He struggled to grapple with the awful truth of it. "But you're freed. Mr. Lincoln signed a paper that says so, turned it into law."

"Buford Collingwood, he isn't the kind of man to let a piece of paper dictate what he believes. What he owns is his—for life."

Douglas reached out and captured her hands. "Philadelphia's a long way off."

"Not far enough, not while there are ships as fast as the *Intrepid*."

"I'll go away with you, then." He added with difficulty, "If you want me."

She gazed at him in wonder. "I can't let you do that, Dougie. Your life is here, your job and the Sinclairs."

"It's not much of a life."

"Your dreams are here." She gestured wildly up the

shore. "Like that house Mr. Sinclair built. That's what you want."

Was it? Maybe—maybe his heart wanted a home. But his heart now beat for Josie.

"Josie, I want that with you."

"Oh, Dougie, sweet Jesus!" Her hands tried to fly up to her face; gently, he restrained them.

"I want to build you a house like that. I want to work my whole life for you. I'm talking about marriage."

"Marriage! To me?"

Was that dismay Douglas heard in her voice? Horror? Before he could decide, she rushed on, "But you know who—what I am."

"I believe I do," Douglas replied. "That's why I'm asking."

****

Josie sat perfectly still with her hands trapped between Dougie's fingers and her heart trapped by his words. He thought he knew; he didn't guess the half of it. If she told him…

She gave an inward, half-hysterical laugh. The man supposed the fact that he'd been born a bastard a terrible thing. Shame stained her cheeks just imagining how much worse he'd consider what she was.

She parted her lips to tell him how impossible it was; the words wouldn't come. Because what he held out to her was just so beautiful. Was it what she wanted? Marriage, children, a life here in a snug, little home, even if it wasn't as pretty as the Sinclairs'. Maybe. A place in this man's heart?

Oh yes, yes, *yes*.

But shouldn't she tell him all, before she accepted

the gift he held out to her? If she did, would he turn away from her? It would be more than she could bear.

"Dougie," she whispered. "People would never accept it. I'm a Negress."

"So? I'm half Indian. They've accepted me, more or less. What choice do they have?"

"This is different."

"Josie, I don't see how."

Again, she tried to draw her hands from his; gently, he retained them, the warmth of him stealing through her. What would it be like to lie in his arms, to feel that warmth in her bed?

Desperately, she said, "You haven't lived what I've lived."

"You're right, I haven't."

"And these men after us—they could come here, steal me away, any time."

"You think I'd let them?" He stared at her. "You think I'll allow anyone to harm one hair on your head?"

"How could you fight them, Dougie? One man…"

"With everything I have. With everything I am."

He raised one of her hands to his lips, kissed the back of it, and turned it over to kiss the palm, then followed by blessing the other hand in the same way.

"Trust me, Josie."

Trust was hard for her. She'd trusted her ma once, when she told Josie everything would be all right. She trusted Daniel, Michael, and Eunice—but she'd be saying farewell to them, staying with this man.

He bowed his dark head over her hands. "Please, Josie."

Following the bidding of her heart, she tumbled forward and into his arms.

Chapter Seven

"Daniel, I won't be going with you on up to the settlement."

Dawn had barely broken on the morning of departure when Josie followed the old man out into the yard, so she might catch him alone on his way back from the "wee hoosie." She didn't want Michael or Eunice to hear—not yet. She imagined her brother would have a few things to say about her decision.

Daniel stopped short and turned his wise gaze upon her. For several heartbeats he didn't speak; then his brow furrowed. "It's that young man, isn't it? Young Master Grier. I saw how it was between the two of you. But girl, that doesn't mean you should stay."

Josie twisted her fingers in her apron. "Yes, Daniel, I believe it does."

Slowly and very reluctantly, Daniel shook his head. "Josie, I'm afraid I have to advise against it."

"Don't you like him?"

"I like him well enough. He's upright and respectful. Been generous to us."

"So?"

"Do I have to say it out straight, girl? He's white."

"Half." Josie's heart beat a tattoo in her throat. "So am I—half."

Daniel nodded somberly. He knew what had gone on in the big plantation house—all of it. "Not in the eyes of the world you're not, girl."

"This isn't the world, just one small town."

"You think that makes a difference? What about those men chasing after us?"

"He says he'll protect me."

Daniel laughed, an incredulous sound. "Can't. They find you, they'll take you."

"Don't say that." Josie's worst nightmare, being dragged back to the plantation or to whatever other place Massa Collingwood now lived. She shivered in the cool morning air.

"Honey, I can't tell you what to do—I ain't your papa."

"Yes, Daniel. Yes, you are."

"And you're a woman grown now. All I'm saying is, you stand a better chance not getting found up in Nova Scotia."

"He says he's willing to come with me."

"Well then."

"But that would mean him giving up everything—his job, his place, and his friends. He thinks he has no roots here, but he does. He just doesn't see it." She swallowed. "He has a lot to lose."

"More than freedom?"

"Surely Massa Collingwood won't send men so far. He has to give up eventually. Daniel, what should I do?"

"How do you feel, child?"

"Like I'm standing on the edge of a cliff ready to jump off."

Daniel smiled. "No, I mean what do you *feel*, girl, inside?"

Josie closed her eyes and stood breathing in the

morning air, groping internally before opening herself within. She felt...the ties that already bound her and Dougie together, glowing bright as certainty.

She opened her eyes and regarded Daniel. "Guess I'm staying."

He laid one gnarled hand on her cheek. "Then, child, you have my blessing."

****

A hard leave-taking, and no mistake. Half a dozen times Douglas feared Josie, standing on the dock beside him, would change her mind and board the *Intrepid*. Every time another box or bundle was carried aboard he had to keep himself from catching her arm and holding her back from following.

This had to be her decision, her choice, free and clear. But her brother hadn't made it easy for her, railing at her loud enough to be heard in the forge after he found out, and then laying on the guilt. *How will Eunice and Hetty manage without you in a strange place? And what about Daniel? It's your place to look after him when he gets old.*

Josie had mollified him at last with words that chilled Douglas to the heart.

"I can always follow after you, Michael, if this doesn't work out."

Even now, standing beside Josie on the wharf and watching as the *Intrepid* sailed out of the harbor, he smarted over those words. Was that truly how she felt? He'd thought her completely committed to what lay between them and to making a future with him.

He stole a look at her, and his heart softened. Tears poured down her face like rain. He tried to imagine how it would feel to watch everyone he knew and loved sail away.

Almost everyone.

He would have to be more to her now, would have to be her whole world. A frightening thought, since he'd never really lived for anybody except himself. That had been hard enough.

How much harder to take this fragile bird into his hands? Well, but if he couldn't protect her, he had to believe his love could.

That was what he felt for her: love the likes of which he'd never imagined. And she must love him too, else she'd be on that ship she now watched out of sight. He needed to remember that.

When nothing was visible on the cloudy horizon, he turned and touched her shoulder. "Come on."

She palmed the tears from her cheeks. "What now?"

"Now we ask for advice. Let's go see Mrs. Sinclair."

Josie had met Lisbeth Sinclair once, when Lisbeth stopped by the blacksmith shop one afternoon. So far they had only a passing acquaintance. Followed by more than one curious gaze, Douglas now led Josie away from the harbor—away from her whole past—and to the little house that overlooked the sea.

Chieftain greeted them when they drew near and led them through the tumbled flowers to the front door, which stood open to the humid morning. Even as they approached Douglas could hear the two boys, Archie and Alasdair, kicking up a fuss. Barely a year separated them in age, and Lisbeth often said they should have been twins, alike as they were with their black hair and mischievous natures.

Douglas couldn't count the scrapes they'd been in, and into which Rab had needed to wade to rescue them. He also knew Rab's heart beat for them, along with Lisbeth and Dorothea.

A frightening thing, he reflected now, letting your heart stray outside your body and start beating for someone else.

He eyed the woman beside him as they waited for Lisbeth to answer the door. Would they have a crop of children together? Was he man enough to protect them all?

Lisbeth smiled when she saw them, with what looked like genuine pleasure. "Douglas, come in. Or, as Rab would say, 'come away in.' " Just like Douglas, Lisbeth had over the years acquired a number of colloquialisms by association. Now she ran a swift look over both him and Josie, and marked the traces of tears on Josie's cheeks.

"Please don't mind the mess," she bade. "I'm just clearing away breakfast. Would you like some?"

"Oh, ma'am." Josie pressed her hands to her stomach. "Thank you, but I don't think I could."

"Tea, then." Lisbeth smiled again. "Dora, put the kettle back on the hob."

She led them into the big kitchen with its scrubbed pine table, where it appeared a storm had blown through. Used dishes cluttered the tabletop, and the drain board, as well; a pot of herbs had been overturned on the windowsill, and toys littered the floor.

Chieftain, who'd followed them in, calmly inserted himself beneath the table, where he began to eat from what looked like a puddle of spilled oatmeal.

Dorothea, standing at the hearth, turned and smiled

at them.

"Here, Miss Freeman, sit down." Lisbeth hastily cleared a place at the table. "Is everything all right?"

"The *Intrepid* just sailed," Douglas explained. "Josie stayed behind. With me."

"Oh!" The gasp came from Dorothea, whose lips formed a perfect O.

For just a moment, Lisbeth looked nonplussed. Then she reached out and touched Josie's hand where it rested on the tabletop. "Oh, my dear, how monumental for you."

Josie nodded, far more wretchedly than Douglas liked.

"And how blindingly romantic!" Dorothea breathed.

The smile that had the power to touch Douglas's soul broke across Josie's face. She nodded again. "It is that, miss."

"Dorothea." The girl came and sat across from Josie. "You must call me that, or Dora. We're going to be friends."

Josie nodded yet again; tears once more flooded her eyes.

"How old are you? I'm thirteen," Dora said proudly. "You can't be that much older."

"Dora, don't pester Miss Freeman," Lisbeth cautioned.

"No, ma'am, honestly I don't mind. I'm nineteen," Josie told Dorothea. "Only just."

"We'll be best friends," Dorothea decided. "I shall call you 'Jo.' It's one of my favorite names."

"Hush now, Dora," Lisbeth bade. "Alasdair and Archie, you take Chieftain out in the yard. Dora, will you please do up the dishes so we might talk?"

The boys went out back, where they promptly began playing noisily. Dorothea obediently got up and gathered the dirty dishes.

Lisbeth gave Josie time to settle while she made tea and set the cups in front of them along with a plate of biscuits. She then took the bench Dorothea had vacated.

"There now. What can I do for you?"

Douglas had once considered Lisbeth Sinclair the prettiest woman he knew—Josie, his Josie, had now supplanted her, though, in his estimation. But Lisbeth had soft, ash-blonde hair and dreamy, blue-gray eyes that belied a very practical nature beneath. And she had a heart nearly as kind as her husband's.

He cleared his throat. "I'm hoping you can advise us the best way to go about this thing," he confessed.

"This thing?"

Josie palmed still more tears. "We've just jumped off a cliff." She stole a look at Douglas. "Holding hands."

"Ah."

Douglas said, "I want everything to be right and proper. Till we're married, I mean."

"Oh!" Dorothea exclaimed again and dropped the oatmeal pot with a clang.

Lisbeth, bless her heart, didn't so much as blink.

"People will talk," Douglas pressed on. "Well, they're going to talk anyway." They'd talked about him all his life. How much more ammunition they would have now!

"Yes, well," Lisbeth said easily, "the thing you have to remember about gossip, it's the product of small minds. People who can't think of anything better or more worthy to occupy them talk about other people."

With absolute certainty Douglas said, "That doesn't make it sting any less."

"True."

"Josie, here, can go on living at the quarters behind the forge."

Without hesitation, Lisbeth offered, "And you can continue to stay here, Douglas."

Josie swiveled her head and looked at him. "This is where you've been sleeping?"

"Only," Douglas went on, "folks might say I went creeping back there even when I didn't—now her family's gone."

Dorothea abandoned her dishes and came to the table. "Not if Jo stays here with us in place of you. She can share my room. And, heck, we're so respectable nobody will blink an eye. Then, once you're married, Jo can go home."

Josie shot Lisbeth a glance, hopeful and measuring. "Oh, I couldn't expect…"

"You're not expecting, we're offering." Lisbeth smiled at her daughter. "I think that's a fine idea."

Douglas let out his breath with a whoosh.

Dorothea leaned on the table. "Jo, do you have a wedding dress? Oh, Ma—how about that white dress you were making when the order got cancelled? It's almost done."

"So it is." Lisbeth answered Josie's questioning look with the explanation, "I'm a seamstress, you see— I work here out of the house."

Dorothea beamed, "She'll look so beautiful."

"So she will," Lisbeth agreed.

Douglas, too grateful to speak, remained silent.

Josie cast him a desperate look. "I'll need a job, though. I can't just live on other people's charity."

"As for that, how are you with a needle?" Lisbeth asked. "I've been considering taking someone on."

The breathtaking smile broke across Josie's face once more. "Mrs. Sinclair, ma'am, sewing's one of the things I do best."

Chapter Eight

Josie, still clad in her white lace gown, stood surveying the quarters behind the forge with new eyes. Hers now—her home.

Someone had come in and cleaned from top to bottom—probably Mrs. Sinclair and Dora, maybe with help from Mrs. Becker and her daughter, Bessie. They had been so good to Josie, she couldn't think about it without welling up.

She repeated it in her mind, so she would believe it. *Her home, her own.*

Just like the man who now stood behind her, so close she could feel his body heat.

He'd insisted on carrying her in—carrying her over the threshold, he called it—and had set her down just inside the door. She knew if she turned around she'd be in his arms.

Where she wanted to be.

They'd been married late this afternoon and had gone back to the Sinclairs' for cake and some drinks. Now dark had nearly fallen, and Lisbeth had chased them home.

Home.

Just her and Dougie, her new husband, alone for the whole night. Heaven.

She'd already kissed him, of course—once at the church, and before that stolen kisses on the rocks where they liked to sit above the bay, and once or twice here in the yard. Josie knew she could get lost in Dougie's kisses, deep and dark as velvet streaked by fire. But she could only imagine what came after the kisses.

He reached out and turned her to him with gentle hands. Her gaze met his, and she tumbled in, losing all her trepidation.

"Let me look at you," he murmured. "So beautiful."

"Am I?" She plucked at her lace skirt. "I never expected to wear such a dress." Miss Alice had owned dozens of them. Josie had brushed them, ironed and mended them, but had never so much as tried one on, even though she and Alice were almost the same size.

Dougie said, "It's not the dress. It's you." Tenderly, he caught her face between his hands and bent his head. Behind his broad shoulders, now clad in a borrowed coat, Josie caught a glimpse of darkening sky dancing with a raft of stars. Then his warm lips found hers in a kiss so sweet it made her ache.

"Josie Grier," he told her then, "I love you."

"And I love you, Mr. Douglas Grier."

"I want to show you."

"Well, seeing as we're proper married, I think you should. But first you'd better shut the door."

He did, right before carrying her to the bed.

****

The hoot of an owl roused Douglas from the depths of sleep sometime near dawn. Starlight still trickled in through the back windows of his quarters, enough to let him orient himself. He was home, in his bed.

Not alone.

Emotion rose up in him, enough to steal his

breath—amazement, wonder, desire, gratitude. Mainly gratitude. Josie loved him. She'd given herself to him, forsaking all others.

How could a man live up to such a gift, to such trust? Especially him, Douglas Grier—bastard son of the town whore—who'd never been worth much.

Lying there in the almost-dark, he drew a breath. Whatever he'd been in the past, he now needed to measure up, because Josie had placed her heart in his keeping, and he dared not stumble. This thing had been miraculous from the start—that he should be called upon to aid her and her family on that night, that the *Intrepid* should founder off the coast of Lobster Cove and throw them back together. That she should agree to forsake all others for *his* sake.

It made him feel at once humble and empowered, engaged in his life as never before.

Josie seemed so small and fragile to make up the better part of his world. He'd been half afraid of breaking her when he'd loved her, even though her passion rose to meet his like a tide. They matched in that as in all things. She had to be resilient, given all she had endured.

Upon that thought, he felt her stir, and not wanting her to wake frightened he laid his hand on her stomach just beneath her breasts. Both her hands came up to cover his.

"Dougie?"

"Here, love."

Funny how she called him *Doogie*, the way Rab did. He clasped her in his arms and drew her closer against him.

"I dreamed—"

"What?" he prompted when she paused.

"Thought I was back home."

"You are home, darling."

"I know." She rubbed her cheek against his shoulder, and his heart swelled.

"I thought I was back at the plantation. The night…"

Again she paused; Douglas felt her throat spasm.

"It's all right."

"It's not." She drew a breath. "Dougie, I need to tell you something, something awful you need to know about me. I should have told you before. Before we got married."

What could it be? No matter. He told her, "I hope you know you can tell me anything."

"But this—this might change how you feel about me. That's why I should have told you first."

Douglas shifted in the bed so he could look into her face. What did he see in her wide, dark eyes? Fear. Horror.

"Massa Collingwood—he's the man who owns me. *Owned* me."

"I know who he is."

"He—"

Again she paused and swallowed convulsively. She studied Douglas's face intently by the dim light, as if measuring his soul.

In a rush she said then, "He's a terrible, cruel man, and he—" She clutched at Douglas with tense hands, and her eyes filled with tears.

"Say it, Josie," he begged. "Just say it." *Trust me.*

"He sold my ma. She worked for him all her life long, lived in that house with him and his wife and daughter, worked her fingers to the bone, and…and she defied him once. *Once.* He sold her away that very day, bundled her off on a wagon by nightfall. I never saw her again."

"Oh, sweetheart." He enfolded her in his arms, wishing he could take away all the hurt, suffer it on her behalf if need be.

She stumbled on, the words half smothered against the naked skin of his throat. "He treated her just like she didn't matter, even though she…she…"

"Was your ma? Are you worrying that'll happen to you? It won't, Josie, it won't. You're safe here with me."

"Are you sure?"

"I'm sure. Josie, listen to me: I'm right here with you now. And nothing can ever change how I feel about you."

"Nothing?"

"No, I promise. Shall I prove it to you?"

Against his shoulder, she nodded.

With his whole body and all his heart, he did.

Chapter Nine

Josie sat in the patch of sunlight coming in through the Sinclairs' front window, setting tiny stitches along the hem of a dark green dress. Nearly four weeks had passed since her wedding, each day like a separate little gift and each night a dream. Half the time she felt as if she danced between joy and despair, the way water dances on a hot griddle, sure of only one thing.

She'd never imagined loving anybody the way she loved her new husband.

And the ties between them—the ties that had formed went deep. They strengthened every morning when he smiled at her and each night when he took her in his arms.

She glanced up from her painstaking work—she would give Mrs. Sinclair only her best—to gauge the afternoon. A bright, windy day with what Dougie called white horses riding on the deep blue ocean, it held a crisp chill that hinted of autumn.

Josie could only try to imagine autumn in this far, northern place, and winter—winter spent wrapped in Dougie's love.

Would she be here still? Seemed she couldn't quite believe it even yet.

Voices coming from outside distracted her from her thoughts. The house seemed busy today, with a steady stream of customers. Plus the children had just come in from school, the two boys racing around in their usual fashion and Dorothea wanting to talk.

Josie smiled involuntarily at the thought of Dora, with her bright conversation and confiding ways. Dora said she wanted to write stories; in fact she insisted someday she would write the story of Josie and Douglas, so everyone could know about their great love.

Douglas. He would still be at work in the forge, strong and skillful, but she'd see him soon. Did he think of her?

Her longing was interrupted when Mrs. Sinclair and her latest customer, Mrs. Mayer, entered the big front room from the porch where they'd been standing, Mrs. Sinclair with her arms full of garments.

Josie had seen Mrs. Mayer in town from time to time. In her fifties, she had a narrow, pinched face and often looked as if she could smell something unsavory.

"You're sure you can get that mending done quick, Lisbeth?"

Lisbeth Sinclair nodded reassuringly. "Oh yes, Bertha, especially now that I have an extra pair of hands."

"Oh." Mrs. Mayer glanced at Josie where she sat before leaning closer to Lisbeth. Just as if Josie weren't right there in the room she said, "Well, but I don't want *her* touching my clothing."

Dismay poured through Josie and settled in the pit of her stomach. Her bright needle faltered. She'd already encountered that sort of attitude in town during the last weeks, mostly in the way folks stared when she and Dougie walked together. At the grocer's, the proprietor had at first been reluctant to serve her, till

Dougie set him straight.

But the last thing she wanted was to damage business for Lisbeth Sinclair, who'd been so good to her.

She felt rather than saw Lisbeth stiffen. In a voice like ice, Lisbeth said, "I assure you, Bertha; Mrs. Grier's sewing is as good as or better than my own."

"It's not *that*." Mrs. Mayer leaned still nearer. Did she really imagine Josie couldn't hear? "I have to wear these things."

Lisbeth withdrew slightly. "Then perhaps you had better take your custom elsewhere."

Three things happened then, all at once: Mrs. Sinclair thrust the bundle of garments toward Mrs. Mayer, the boys burst into the room with Chieftain in tow, and Dorothea descended the stairs like an avenging angel.

Two flags of color flew in Dorothea's cheeks, and her first words made it clear she'd overheard. "Mrs. Mayer, that's just pure meanness on your part, it is! Why wouldn't you want Jo touching your things? She's an expert seamstress, so my ma says."

"Dorothea," Lisbeth cautioned.

Mrs. Mayer drew herself up, the familiar look of distaste coming over her face again. "What business is it of yours, Dorothea Sinclair?"

"Well, I'll tell you, shall I? Douglas Grier is like a brother to me, and that makes his wife, Jo, my sister. And I'm proud to say she's also fast becoming my friend. If you're so nasty and narrow-minded you can't see—"

"Dorothea!" Lisbeth snapped in a voice Josie had never before heard her employ.

Dorothea buttoned her lip, but Josie could see it went hard with her.

Josie stumbled to her feet, the green dress dangling from her hands, and stood trembling.

Mrs. Mayer sniffed through her long nose. "Dorothea Sinclair, you are a rude child. I think your parents should be ashamed of you speaking in such a way to your elders."

"Proud, you mean," Lisbeth retorted. "I am very proud of my daughter." She finished depositing the bundle of clothing in Mrs. Mayer's arms. "I'm afraid, Mrs. Mayer, I will have to refuse your custom."

"High and mighty, are you?" Mrs. Mayer frowned and flicked a look at Josie where she stood. "With *that* in your parlor."

Lisbeth made a sweeping gesture to the open door. Alasdair, Archie, and Chieftain, who stood frozen in front of it, quickly moved aside. "Mrs. Mayer, you are most welcome to leave."

Nose in the air, Mrs. Mayer did. The silence became so complete Josie could hear the woman's feet crunching on the gravel path as she stalked away, and the waves slapping down on the shore.

"Ma?" Archie queried then.

"It's all right, lads. Go play till suppertime. Just make sure you keep Chieftain with you if you go down on the rocks."

"Ma," Dorothea echoed her brother as soon as the two boys had gone. "I don't see any call for you to scold me—"

"It wasn't what you said, Dorothea, but the way you said it. No need for you to point out all the flaws in her nasty personality quite so directly. Well!" Lisbeth drew a breath. "That will be all over town before the sun sets."

"I'm sorry," Josie began.

Lisbeth fixed her with a level stare. "For what? Not your fault, honey, that the woman's a shrew. She's one of the ones spread gossip about Rab and me before we were married, while I was staying where you're living now—even though Rab bunked elsewhere. However"—she switched her gaze to her daughter—"that doesn't mean we can go around insulting folks."

Dorothea tilted up her chin. "Even her?"

"Even her," Lisbeth said firmly.

"But," Josie again attempted, "if me being here is going to cost you customers…"

"Just let folks get a gander at the quality of your sewing," Lisbeth assured her, "and we'll see how business increases. And that embroidery you can do—I was thinking of making that a specialty, and charging a pretty penny, too. If you're willing, that is."

Josie nodded and gave a wobbly smile. "I purely enjoy doing embroidery," she confessed.

"Well, then," Lisbeth declared, "I don't suppose we need Mrs. Mayer's business."

Josie sank back into her seat, and Lisbeth eyed her kindly.

"Dorothea, go put the kettle on."

With a final glare down the pathway, Dorothea went.

****

"I missed you," Dougie said.

Josie could tell. He'd come straight from the forge when he heard her arrive home, dressed as she best liked to see him, in the leather apron that showed off his

63

shoulders and muscular back, still all warm and glistening from his place beside the fire. She moved into his arms, and some of the hurt from the afternoon fell away.

Some.

He drew her closer. Josie loved the way Dougie touched her, like he thought she might shatter in his hands. She remembered how she'd seen Massa Collingwood touch women, her ma and later Eunice, with rough demand.

But she didn't want to think about Buford Collingwood, especially now.

She smiled up at her husband. "I'll get supper started right away."

"I'm not hungry. Leastwise—well, darling, you know what I want."

Josie looked into his dark eyes and promptly melted. She knew, and it made her pulse race.

"Here, now, you're not going to need that heavy apron." She stretched up on her tiptoes and untied it from around his neck. "You sure are a beautiful man, Douglas Grier. It's like you were made perfect, just for me."

She ran her palms over his now naked chest and felt him catch fire.

"Never knew why I was in the world," he confessed, "but that might just be it."

He kissed her so her toes curled and she had to hold onto him in order to stay upright. Then he whispered into her neck, "I've been thinking about you. All day."

If that was so, then nothing else mattered—so long as they were together and the rest of the world stayed beyond the door.

"Well, then," she whispered back, "I reckon you'd better do something about it."

He did, removing her clothing one piece at a time and chasing each garment with a kiss. By the time he carried her to their bed she barely remembered Mrs. Mayer's name.

Later, dazed and still tingling, she lay and thought about what he'd said. She, too, had often wondered why she was in the world. Her presence had never seemed to mean much to anyone save her family.

Maybe it was all for this—so the two of them, both drifting lost, could find a harbor and a home in one another.

"Dougie, you awake?"

She'd meant to tell him about Mrs. Mayer and the way the Sinclair women had stood up for her. Now though, the quiet dark had fallen outside, and she felt far too much peace to dredge all that up again. Besides, something else needed to be said.

"Umm?" he replied, more than half asleep and with his wavy dark hair messed up on the pillow. Sweet lord, he looked so handsome, and his heart beat so true. What had she ever done to deserve this little piece of heaven? And about to get better, at least she hoped he'd think so.

"I missed my monthly."

"Eh?"

"We've been married almost four weeks. And it should have come last Tuesday."

He lifted his bent arm from his forehead and stared at her. "What should?"

"My monthly, Dougie. My woman's time. Don't

you know what I'm talking about?"

She could tell the instant he did. His stare intensified, and sheer joy shone at her from his eyes.

"You mean—?"

She nodded.

Reverently, he laid his big, warm hand on her belly. "Already?"

"Well, I guess, Dougie Grier, when two people are this perfect for each other, it doesn't take long."

Chapter Ten

"Some men are here, new arrived in town, and asking after you." Ed Becker said the words baldly, but Douglas, looking up from his work, saw concern in the man's eyes.

Douglas liked Ed Becker—the Beckers were good friends to Rab and Lisbeth. Ed's wife Frannie managed their big family with warmth and humor, and Ed worked as hard as anyone at Sawyer's mill. In fact it wasn't like him to leave off and come by so early.

Rab glanced up from the workbench with sudden attention. "What men are these?"

Ed shrugged. "Didn't rightly say. Three of 'em came in on the packet boat this morning from Bar Harbor, and I didn't much like the look of them. They ain't been here yet?"

Rab shook his head. "No."

"Seem to be making the rounds of businesses. Thing is," Ed looked at Douglas again, apologetically, "when I say they're asking after you, I mean more exactly they're asking after your wife."

Douglas's heart clenched and fell to his feet. It felt just like getting punched in the stomach; for a minute he couldn't catch his breath.

No, God, not that.

Rab went quickly to shut the shop door before coming to the anvil where Douglas had been working.

"Where is she, Dougie?"

"At work—your place up the shore."

"Good. Out of the way." Rab squeezed Ed's shoulder. "You didn't tell them anything?"

"No, course not. But somebody might. They're going all 'round, as I say. And they're offering a reward for word of her—said some relation's looking for her, but I didn't believe it. Who are they, Douglas?"

"Slave hunters."

"What? There's no such thing as slaves in this country anymore."

"Bounty hunters, then, sent to find folk and drag them back where they came from."

"But," Ed sputtered, "little Josie's your wife now, right and legal."

"Doesn't matter. They don't follow the law, see, don't consider it legitimate." Douglas set his hammer down on the bick very carefully so it wouldn't snap in his hands.

He raised his eyes to Ed. "Reckon there are people in Lobster Cove might just take their part. Some never wanted Josie here." Never much wanted him here, either—a thing he'd learned early and felt ever since he'd been old enough to understand. "They've made their opinion clear, too."

Ed looked shocked. "But that's a far different thing from letting her be dragged away by these fellows. Nobody in Lobster Cove would—"

In the face of Douglas's stare, his words died away. He swallowed. "Son, you really believe that?"

Douglas shrugged stiffly. "I'm not about to take any chances. I promised Josie I'd protect her, and that's what I'll do no matter what it takes." Did this man—

Buford Collingwood, so Josie called him—really think he could send his agents to snatch Douglas's wife? And his tiny unborn child with her, a child he might never see if these arrogant bastards had their way.

Rab gave a hard nod. "Go to her now, Dougie. Leave out the back. You have to warn her. Best if she stays put for the time being, till we can determine what's what." He removed his leather apron and snatched up his shirt. "Ed and I will go find these fellows, see if we can apply a little friendly dissuasion."

"That should be my job."

"Will be, son, if they prove too stubborn," Ed said. "Let us talk to them first."

Dougie nodded, stripped off his own apron, and snatched his shirt from the peg on the wall. He'd go, right enough—with Josie was where he wanted to be.

But how could he give her such news? By God, how could he speak those words?

****

"So, Mrs. Applegate wants to submit my story to the contest administrators in Augusta. She thinks I have a very good chance of winning."

Lisbeth exchanged looks with Josie and smiled. Josie smiled back, even though she hadn't been listening as closely as she should. She shifted in her seat, trying to lose the uneasy feeling that had plagued her ever since she'd arrived at the Sinclairs' house this morning. Felt almost like a storm coming even though the day stayed bright and sunny. This storm hovered only in the back of her mind.

She pushed the nebulous worry away once again and tried to focus on what Dorothea had to say. Usually she loved listening to Dora's chatter, and this must be important since she'd been talking about the story contest from the time she got home from school, all while both women sat sewing.

"Well," Lisbeth said decisively, "you do tell a fine story. I don't doubt you have a good chance."

"Once my writing course arrives from the institute in Augusta, I'll be able to polish my work and make it that much better." Perched on the sofa, Dorothea swung one foot. "Ma, I've told Jo I want to write her story. I mean, it's a tale that needs to be told. I'll send it to one of those big publishers in Boston, just like Louisa May Alcott."

"Don't get ahead of yourself, sweetheart." Lisbeth bit off a thread. "Maybe Josie doesn't want folks peering into her life."

"But she's a true heroine. And her story's so romantic." Dorothea sighed.

Josie smiled again. "I think I'd just as soon stay in the background, Dora. The fewer people know I'm here the better. And I do believe Dougie would prefer that, as well."

"Speak of the Devil." Lisbeth glanced out the door, which stood open to the sunshine. "Isn't that him now?"

"What's he doing here this time of day?"

Dorothea clasped her hands melodramatically. "Probably missed you."

But as soon as Josie got a look at Dougie's expression, she knew that wasn't it. Tense and strained, the sweat stood out upon him as if he'd run all the way up the shore.

Josie's heart plummeted and she surged to her feet, her sewing dropping from her hands. The foreboding inside her came together with a rush, and just like that she knew the truth; she spoke even before he could.

"They're here, aren't they? The slave hunters. They've come."

****

"I think it's best if you stay here." Lisbeth had turned pale as milk, and her eyes looked too big for her face. "We can hide you upstairs or in the barn out back." She glanced at Douglas. "Tell her."

Douglas, all the careful words he'd rehearsed stolen from him, reached out and seized his wife's hands. She looked frantic, as if she'd fly to pieces. He supposed that was how a woman looked when a terrifying past—or her worst nightmare—caught up with her.

"Listen, Josie, listen to me."

She stilled, but barely. Her eyes were wild and her fingers icy.

"I won't stay here and have those men down upon Lisbeth and Dora. Someone's bound to say I work here. They'll tear this pretty house apart."

"You think I mind about the house?" Lisbeth snapped. "It's wood and mortar."

"You love this house," Josie wailed. "Mr. Sinclair put his heart in it, and…"

Lisbeth made a swift decision. "Douglas, take her up the shore to the old O'Shea place. You know where it is?"

Douglas nodded. "I do. But, ma'am, I can't do that. I mean to face these men down." To stand between them and the woman he loved.

Lisbeth gave him a long look and nodded. "Dorothea, you take Josie to the cottage. Take Chieftain and the lads with you—those boys couldn't keep quiet about anything if their lives depended on it. Chieftain will protect you if it comes to it. Douglas, you go back to town. If those men do learn Josie works here, maybe you and Rab can persuade them away."

That meant he had to leave Josie—only to defend her, yes, but it hurt impossibly all the same.

He looked her in the eyes and, quivering, she threw herself into his arms.

With part of his attention he heard Lisbeth call Dorothea away, affording them a moment alone.

One moment.

"Oh God, God, God—" Josie wailed. "I prayed this day would never come. How I prayed! What if they find me and take me away? What if I never see you again?"

"Won't happen. Can't happen. I promised you, didn't I? Josie—Josie, look at me."

She raised her face to him, her eyes swimming with tears.

"Josie, you remember those chains and shackles I broke off you that night? How heavy they were, how tight?"

She nodded. Two tears trickled down.

Intently, he told her, "Those were nothing—*nothing*—to the ties that bind us together now. Those were made out of hate. But the ones between you and me—well, they were forged by love. And there's nothing stronger—not in this world or the next. You understand?"

Her lips trembled before she formed the word, "Yes."

"Doesn't matter if I'm back in town and you're up the shore—those ties aren't going to break. And those men won't take you, Josie, not while I'm still breathing."

He kissed her then, a kiss into which he poured all his devotion. It seemed to afford her strength, for she pulled herself together and steadied beneath his hands.

"Now go. Dorothea's waiting." He gestured to the kitchen doorway where Dorothea hovered, having no doubt heard all.

Josie nodded again before she wrenched herself from his arms and ducked out through the kitchen, looking over her shoulder at him only once.

It was the hardest thing he'd ever done, to stand and watch her go.

Chapter Eleven

Those men won't take you, Josie—not while I'm still breathing. Dougie's promise repeated over and over in Josie's mind as she followed Dorothea up the shore with the lads and Chieftain following, Alasdair and Archie laughing and playing as if this were some game. She little knew or cared where they were going.

The discord that had grown within her all day while she sat quietly stitching had culminated in a storm of terrible proportions. Oh, why had she failed to listen to that inner voice, the one that spoke to her at the very worst—and very best—of times? She'd sat there like a fool while the slave hunters sailed into Lobster Cove harbor ready to destroy her life.

She stumbled over a stone on the seldom-used path and just caught herself from falling. Chieftain, the big Newfoundland dog, pushed up to her side and looked at her with what seemed like concern. Would he protect her? Just like her Dougie.

Those men won't take you, Josie—not while I'm...

She halted his comforting voice in her head as a new thought hit her, so terrible it froze her in her tracks. *Not while I'm still breathing.*

But what if Dougie—her beloved husband with the strong, gentle hands and the bottomless dark eyes and that rare, beautiful smile—stopped breathing? What if those awful men who followed her made it so? They were violent and merciless, capable of killing anybody who stood between them and their quarry. She'd heard the stories. And Dougie was but one man.

Oh, Lord, what if she'd just sent him to his death? Darkness overcame her in a wave, and she swayed where she stood.

"Jo?"

Dorothea stopped on the path ahead; even the boys paused and stood, for once, quiet.

"Are you all right?"

"I need to go back."

Dorothea looked appalled. For once she groped for words before she said, "You can't! It's too dangerous."

"I don't care."

"Let Douglas see them off."

"But he—I can't let him risk himself for my sake."

Dorothea came back a few steps and touched Josie's hand. "Why not? He lives for your sake, doesn't he?"

Josie met Dorothea's eyes—such dreamy-looking eyes for such a levelheaded young lady. "Maybe."

"Listen to me, Jo. I've known Douglas Grier all my life. I've never seen him as happy as he's been with you. *Never*. Let him protect you. It's his right."

"He's just one man." Josie said starkly, "They might kill him."

"Come on." Dorothea tugged Josie's hand. "We can't stand out here in the open. It's not much farther now."

Torn, Josie hovered between the pull of the girl's fingers and the one, far stronger, that drew her back toward Lobster Cove. For an instant, she closed her eyes and listened.

Could she feel him? The ties—those he said were stronger than any chains—still connected them.

He lived; he breathed yet.

She allowed Dorothea to pull her on.

****

The town of Lobster Cove, usually as laconic as a Yankee fisherman, now buzzed. The arrival of the packet boat carrying letters and news tended to create a bit of a flurry anyway. Now its passengers—three men the likes of which Douglas had never seen even in his time away in the war—seemed to have infected the place like a contagion.

Folks had abandoned their work, left their homes, and come out into the street, women with baskets and bundles and some with small children in tow, men standing in twos and threes, talking.

The three bounty hunters—for Douglas could think of them as nothing else—had split up and gone about the place, their hard faces set and no mercy in their eyes. Douglas, standing in front of the blacksmith shop, wondered how long it would be before someone spoke of the Freemans and of Douglas's little wife.

He wanted to challenge those men and smash his fists into their faces—wanted it so much he could barely contain himself. He wanted to set them straight and send them packing. But as Rab pointed out, they came heavily armed.

"Wait and see what happens," Rab advised.

Douglas could imagine what would happen. Plenty of folks hadn't been happy having the Freemans in town, and some didn't approve of his marriage to Josie.

Anyway, was anything harder than waiting?

He didn't have to endure it long. Before an hour

passed the searchers made a beeline for the blacksmith shop—not just one but all three of them. They came at a swagger, broad-brimmed hats pushed to the backs of their heads and long coats thrown open to display their weapons.

Douglas, back at his work, looked up from the anvil when they darkened the doorway, and his nerves tightened unbearably.

Josie? He asked in his mind. *You still all right?*

She didn't answer, of course, but he could feel his connection to her holding strong. Safe, then. He drew a breath.

"Lookin' for Douglas Grier," said the first man through the door, in a drawl. He sported a large handlebar moustache and had small eyes, easily the coldest Douglas had ever seen.

Douglas clenched his fingers on the hammer in his hand. "You've found him."

The man pushed his way further into the shop. The other two followed and fanned out, one on either side of him. Douglas felt rather than saw Rab shift over to his side.

"We're after a little Negress," the first man spat. "Hear you might know where she is."

Douglas shook his head.

"Well, now," said the man on the right, "not sure as how we believe that. See, we've been chasing down a band of escaped slaves, and we figure this is the end of the trail, at least for one of 'em. We're taking her, son, and we're taking her today."

"I'm not your son." Rage rose to Douglas's head, so bright he could barely see through it. In the past he'd never stood up for much, never fought very hard on his

77

own behalf—maybe not so hard as he should. That was about to change.

"Goes by the name of 'Josie'—Collingwood or Freeman, take your pick," the third man stated. "That ring a bell?"

"Not here."

The first man glanced behind Douglas at the curtained doorway to the rear quarters. "Find I don't believe that, either. You won't mind if we take a look."

Rab edged forward. "I own this place. I don't just let folks come walking in."

The slave hunter eyed Rab up and down the way he might measure a horse at auction. "No quarrel with you, mister."

Rab jerked his head at Douglas. "You have a quarrel with him, you've got one with me."

Douglas felt a flash of gratitude. But the slave hunter's hand moved toward the pistol on his hip. "Now, mister, you don't want none of this. We're just here to recover some missing property. We know Mr. Collingwood's slaves passed through here and that when they moved on, one of them stayed."

"You're behind the times," Rab said coolly. "No slaves in this country, not any more. We fought a war over it and, *mister*, your side lost."

The first man jerked his head. "Grady, look in back."

"I don't think so." Rab moved to block the way and stood like a rock.

Douglas raised the hammer up onto his shoulder. "Get back on the packet boat while you can still do it under your own power. It's hard for a man to walk when he has two broken legs."

The slave hunter smiled the way Douglas imagined a snake might. "Talk 'round this town says you married this little Negress we're after. So I figure if you married her she must be close by, right?"

"Swear to God," Douglas said thickly, "I'll take you to pieces before I let you touch her."

"Well, son, you may think you have a claim, but—"

"She's my wife."

The man went on, as if Douglas hadn't spoken, "I know a man with a better." He turned his head and looked at his companions. "Go get Mr. Collingwood."

Douglas barked, "Who?" But he knew all too well who Buford Collingwood was, and sickness churned in his gut. "Here?"

The slave hunter gave him another long look before he turned back to his man. "Ask Mr. Collingwood to come speak up for his daughter."

Chapter Twelve

"I need to go back." The words came from Josie as if impelled by some irresistible force impossible to deny.

Dorothea stared at her in alarm. The two of them sat on the floor of the deserted cottage a mile or so up the shore, the place devoid of furnishings, while Chieftain guarded the door and the two lads played some game that led them from room to room.

Dorothea had kept up a steady stream of chatter, to which Josie failed to listen. All the while her inner senses screamed at her, till now, with the sun sinking away to the west and dark gathering off over the sea, she knew what she must do.

"No." Dorothea lowered her voice, maybe in the vain hope the boys wouldn't hear. "You can't! Those men…"

"You think they won't figure it out, discover where I am?"

"Douglas will turn them away."

"No." Violently, Josie shook her head. Oh, she believed in Douglas's promise right enough. But he didn't know the kind of people these were. Josie did, and she'd rather return to Massa Collingwood than see him pay the ultimate price on her behalf.

That's what love was about, wasn't it? Caring more about somebody else than herself. And she cared more, so much more.

He'd given her that promise, sure, but he couldn't keep it if he was no longer breathing. And she couldn't go on living knowing she'd cost him everything.

"If they come here, Dora, they'll hurt you, and the boys, and Chieftain."

The big dog turned his eyes on her and huffed, as if he knew she spoke of him. Both boys stopped their running and came to stand beside their sister. They eyed Josie gravely.

Josie so seldom saw them still, or quiet, it seemed strange now. They had handsome little faces, dark hair, and their father's deep blue eyes, gone solemn.

Josie's heart clenched with protective love. She couldn't let harm come to them for her sake. She had to go and face this nightmare that had followed her so long, had to face it down.

She scrambled up from the dusty floor. "Dora, you stay here with your brothers. I don't want any harm to come to them."

"No," Dorothea said again, and her face went pale and tight. She seized Josie by the wrist. "I don't want any harm to come to you!"

"What is it, Dora?" Alasdair, the elder of the two lads, asked. "What's happening in town?"

Dorothea stood, which brought Chieftain to her side. "Jo, Douglas told you to stay away."

"But he's in danger. I can feel it." Josie pressed her hand to her breast. "Here."

"Oh, God," Dorothea whispered, "I don't know what to do."

Josie touched her cheek. "Not up to you, Dora. This is for me to do." To face, at last.

Dorothea pulled Josie close in a fierce hug. "You have to be the bravest person I've ever known."

Funny, Josie didn't feel so brave.

****

She ran as she hadn't run since that awful night when the chains fell from her wrists, not away from the danger this time but into it. The dark slipped over the land from the direction of the sea to accompany her, and her heart pounded in time with her footfalls. Terror sat on her shoulder, an even closer companion.

As she ran she formed a plan in her mind: she would go to the blacksmith shop, enter through the back quarters and see what was what. If Dougie had managed to chase those men off, all well and good. If not, she would have to get between him and them the way a mama cat got between her kittens and a fierce dog. Because she knew just what this kind of men would do.

Dougie had never lived in her world, a place of unreasonable injustice and unfathomable cruelty.

Hadn't she always known things would end this way, with her dragged back into the same nightmare from which she'd emerged? Yes, she'd known this time with Dougie for nothing but a beautiful dream, and just as fleeting.

She pressed one hand to her belly as she ran and wondered about the little one who sheltered there. Dougie's child. Would it be born far away from here and never know its father?

Tears blurred her vision as she pelted on. How hard it was to protect the ones she loved!

The discord inside her unfurled ever more sharply when she reached town, the big dog still loping at her side. She should have begun meeting folks by now, but they passed no one at the harbor or along Main. She ducked behind the houses and businesses that lined Maple, so as to approach the blacksmith's through the back yard. She tore open the door to the quarters which were empty, and froze where she stood.

She could hear voices.

They came at her like blows through the curtain that closed off the forge and from further still—out in the street. Men, angry—shouting. All the agonized warning that had been clamoring inside her surged into one bright spear, sharp as pain.

Dougie's voice. And another that stole her breath and drove her to her knees.

Not that. Not *him*. Not *here*.

Chieftain looked at her in question and moved nearer, panting. Calling upon every shred of will, Josie used the dog's broad back and pushed herself back up.

Driven by the love inside her, she walked through the forge and out into the street.

****

Douglas rarely allowed himself to indulge in hatred. He'd learned all too well by watching Rab Sinclair that a good man instead chose kindness and reason. But the individual who now stood facing him in the middle of the street destroyed all his hard-learned forbearance, swept it away like a harsh wind.

Buford Collingwood. Douglas didn't know what he'd pictured when Josie spoke of her former master, but it wasn't this. A cruel man, yes—hadn't he sold Josie's ma away? Powerful, perhaps. Wealthy, though surely most of what he'd owned before the war must be lost to him now.

To be sure, he retained enough wealth to hire these mercenaries to track innocent folks down, and to book his own passage for the sake of…what? Spite?

Looking into the man's face, Douglas believed it, for his was a face made ugly by hard and bitter emotions, lines carved deep, cheeks sunken. Buford Collingwood did not appear well, his complexion grayed and the fine clothes he wore hanging on a gaunt frame.

Douglas hoped he was dying.

Josie's father. Those words whispered in the back of his mind. And then—no, it couldn't be so. It must be a lie.

She would have told him. Wouldn't she?

Thank God she wasn't here.

"You know who I am," Collingwood said to him now. He had come up from the packet boat led by the fellow called Grady, and Douglas met him in the street with his hammer still in his hand. The four of them now ranged opposite him, the three slave hunters at Collingwood's back.

The entire town, or so it seemed, had gathered, filtering up and standing along the street utterly silent. The last thing Douglas ever wanted was to be a show, but he was willing to fight this out here or anywhere else.

"I know who you are," he spat and barely recognized his own voice, thick with loathing.

"Then you understand I have a prior claim to Josie Collingwood." The man's lip curled. "I understand she goes by the name Josie Freeman now."

"Josie Grier," Douglas said carefully. "You're speaking of my wife."

Collingwood gave a cough of laughter. "You'll have to do better than that. She was born on my land. That makes her my property, just like any other livestock. And no piece of paper signed by any Negro-lover in Washington is going to make me give up what's mine. The laws I obey were made in the Confederacy, son."

"I'm not your son," Douglas returned, as he had earlier.

"Well, then, you can't claim you're married to her, because the little filly's my daughter. By-blow got on one of my house slaves." Collingwood gave a ghastly smile that revealed pale yellow teeth. "Wealth, you see, has its privileges."

A red haze appeared before Douglas's eyes. When it faded, he stood in the grips of several of his neighbors, the hammer raised above his head, and all three of the slave hunters had their weapons drawn, aimed upon him.

Buford Collingwood took a decided step backward and adjusted his fine coat.

"We're taking her, boy, and there's not a damn thing you can do about it—'less you're fixing to die."

"No!" Josie cried as she stepped out into the center of the street.

Chapter Thirteen

For an instant Douglas's world flickered before his eyes as protest racked him. The last thing he wanted to see at that moment was Josie, here. He'd meant to fight this battle for her, had believed her safe up the shore.

He didn't want her to see him die.

But there she came, stepping out with her head high, delicate shoulders squared and terror bright in her eyes. And she'd never looked more beautiful to him.

She took the place beside him, and her fingers slipped into his even as her love slipped around him, a living wall of restraint.

A murmur ran through the crowd. Other than that, it was quiet enough to hear one of the slave hunters cock his gun.

"Well, now, Josie," Collingwood said. "It's time we went home."

"Not with you." She shook her head violently. "My home's not with you."

"It's certainly not here with him."

"He's my husband."

"Yes?" Collingwood sneered. "I suppose you think you've done well, girl, catching yourself a 'breed. Can't you tell that's what he is? Nothing but a dirty, half-breed Indian. I know that just by looking at him."

Douglas flushed as the crowd of onlookers murmured still louder. Yes, likely that was what they considered him, as well, but it didn't matter. Because he could feel Josie's love so strong around him the hurt just fell away.

"I've done well," Josie retorted. "Probably better than I deserve. Far better than you, with your hate and your ugliness, so why don't you just take yourself on out of here and leave me be." She almost shouted it. "Leave me be!"

But Collingwood shook his head. "Not going to happen, girl. It's the principle of the thing, see— nobody takes what belongs to me. Now, unless you want your 'breed shot down in the street like the dog he no doubt is, tell him to step aside, and you come along with me." Deliberately he added, "Daughter."

It was Douglas who moved, stepped in front of Josie and pushed her well behind.

"You'll not take her. You'll have to kill me first. Just remember there are laws for murder, even for killing a *'breed*. You'll find out how it feels to be hunted to your last breath."

Collingwood threw back his head in a blatant show of arrogance. "You think you can stop us, one man alone?"

"He's not alone, though, is he?" Rab Sinclair, solid as a bull and twice as angry, stepped up shoulder-to-shoulder with Douglas, an iron bar in his hands. "I'm here with him."

"As am I." Lisbeth took the place on Douglas's other side, pushing Josie further back as she did. Douglas could feel Lisbeth trembling.

"And me." Ed Becker butted up against Rab, a length of two-by-four in his hands.

"And me."

"Me!"

Folks from the town—people Douglas had never expected to so much as acknowledge him—began flooding forward from all sides, forming a human wall with him at its center and Josie behind. Most were unarmed, some carried whatever they'd been holding when the confrontation began—baskets, bundles, brooms.

Up Maple, from the same direction Collingwood had come, Douglas saw three figures approaching at full tilt. Dorothea, breathless, steamed at their head, for once outdistancing her two brothers.

Lisbeth gasped as all three ran around the men with the cocked guns and threw themselves into the line that stood with Douglas. Chieftain promptly pressed in beside them.

"You'll not hurt her, you evil men!" Dorothea cried breathlessly. "Jo Grier is my friend. So you'll have to go through me to get to her."

"And me." To Douglas's astonishment, Mrs. Mayer, stiff with indignation, took the place at Dorothea's side.

The old woman, eyes narrowed, shook her finger in Buford Collingwood's face. "This is an upright, God-fearing, *northern* town. We don't let bullies come in here doing the Devil's business. Douglas Grier is part of this town and Josie's his wife. So unless you're prepared to shoot a lot of women and children, you'll tell your men to put their guns away, and you'll get on that packet boat and never come back. Because here in Lobster Cove, Maine, we stick together. And you just might find a lobster gaff in your back if you don't go quick enough. Understand?"

Buford Collingwood stared at Bertha Mayer. Neither blinked for several long minutes. Then Collingwood made a harsh gesture for his men to lower their weapons.

"Ma'am, I'll never stand accused of warring against women." He focused his bitter gaze on Douglas for an instant before he snapped, "You're welcome to her, sir—she isn't worth any more of my time."

Douglas sagged where he stood, nearly too relieved to stand. The strong human wall all around him kept him upright, as did the feel of Josie's fingers pressed flat against his back.

That and the joy of Dorothea's chortle as Collingwood called his hounds away and they moved off down the street. "Ha! I guess we told him. Nothing and no one can stand against the citizens of Lobster Cove."

Rab reached out and placed a hand on each of his son's heads. "Ah, but does no one in this family ever do as they're told?"

Chapter Fourteen

"Why didn't you tell me?" Douglas voiced the question softly into the near darkness. He'd followed Josie into the yard when she went out for water, and now they stood with the night insects buzzing all around, only the light from the lamp she'd lit alleviating the velvet softness that closed in.

She dropped the bucket with a thud and leaned against him, her forehead at his heart.

Carefully he repeated, "Why didn't you tell me Collingwood was—"

"My father? I wanted to. I tried. I thought it would change how you felt about me."

"How could it? How could anything?"

"But it's such an ugly, dirty thing. For as long as I could remember, since I was old enough to understand, I knew what I was: a by-blow got on a slave taken to Massa Collingwood's bed against her will. It was one of her duties, like getting up extra early to lay the fires and cook the meals so other folks—better folks—could be warm and fed. My ma wasn't the first or the last. There were others just like me—half white. We didn't matter to him any more than the litters of kittens the barn cats left, 'cept we were worth money."

Douglas cradled her shoulders in his hands and pulled her closer. She still tingled from that scene out in the street, from wonder at how folks had stepped up to defend her. She could scarcely believe Massa—she corrected herself hastily—Mr. Collingwood—had gone for good. Was it over? Was she safe?

But now came the reckoning, admitting the rest of it—all of it—to the man she loved. She gasped, "I was ashamed to tell you."

Very gently he cupped her face and lifted her chin so he could meet her eyes. "You need to believe, darling, nothing will ever change the way I feel about you. But I think, don't you, we should get it all out between us."

Josie swallowed convulsively. "He started using my ma when she was about sixteen. She worked in the kitchen then. He put her in the big house like—like it was a privilege. Serving his wife. His daughter—his proper daughter, Alice—and I were born almost at the same time. My ma nursed both of us."

"Your half-sister. Did she know?"

Josie shrugged helplessly. "Nobody talked about it. There were others besides my ma, but he went back to her again and again."

"Michael?"

Josie smiled wobbily. "Daniel's. Massa—Mr. Collingwood had married Ma to Daniel, his houseman, by then. So things would look proper, like. My ma—she promised me that it would never happen to me. She said she'd got that much assurance from him, that we'd get to stay in the big house, we'd never be sold away, and he'd never use me in his bed."

"I should think not. His own daughter…"

"Doesn't matter. They both lied, Ma and him. My parents. Once Eunice got too big with his child for him to want her in his bed—"

91

"Eunice?"

"Little Hetty's my half-sister too. Anyway, he turned his eye on me. Ma went to him and protested it. First time she ever questioned or refused anything in her whole life. He sold her away that same night. Like I told you, I never saw her again."

"God, Josie! Maybe we can find her. We can look—"

"No." Josie raised her eyes, brimming with tears, to his. "I think she's dead." She pressed her hands to her heart. "I feel it."

Douglas gazed deep into her eyes. "And Collingwood never, he never—"

She shook her head violently. "Never had the chance. A little complication called the Union army distracted him then, and not long after there was the fire. He chained us up that night because he knew the Yankees were coming and he wanted to make sure we didn't get away."

She reached up and touched his face tenderly. "Sure, you know there's never been anybody for me but you, Dougie, from that first night I saw you."

"I know. And nobody for me but you."

"But, Dougie, don't you care what I am? That awful man's blood in my veins…"

"Do you care what I am?" he returned. "Who my parents were?"

"No," she confessed. "Only that you're mine, mine, *mine*."

"Yours forever," he whispered. "And you want to stay here in Lobster Cove to raise our child? We could still follow your family, since I have none."

"How can you say that, Dougie Grier? The

Sinclairs are your family, and you couldn't find finer. Do you believe the way that Dorothea stood up for me?"

A smile tugged at one corner of Dougie's mouth.

"Come to think on it," Josie went on, "seems like you have a whole town full of family ready to claim you for their own—even that Mrs. Mayer."

"I confess, that did surprise me." The smile spread to his eyes. "You know, Josie, I never really thought I belonged here or anywhere. Guess this day has proved me wrong."

"You remember what you said about the ties forged by love, Dougie? They're stronger than anything else. Strong enough to hold you to this place."

"And," he said just before he kissed her, "is love strong enough to chase away the nightmares?"

Josie enjoyed her husband's kiss to the full before she answered. "I'm pretty sure the only dreams from here on out will be beautiful ones."

"That," said Dougie, "is exactly what I wanted to hear."

The White Gull

by

Laura Strickland

The Lobster Cove Series

Chapter One

Frenchman Bay, Maine, September 1851

Lisbeth O'Shea awakened from the depths of sleep abruptly, as if someone had called her name, and opened her eyes. She lay for a moment searching the intense darkness of the room with all her senses.

Outside a storm raged; she could hear wild, ragged waves clawing at the strip of shingle that fronted the cottage, and rain struck the windows intermittently as if someone threw handfuls of gravel at them.

Surely the storm had wakened her, nothing more.

She drew a breath, struggling for it, and tried to calm her racing heart. Was she alone?

Overhead the rafters creaked like the planks of an old ship. The cottage had belonged to the O'Sheas, parents of her late husband, Declan. He had grown up here, the son of a lobster fisherman. How many times had he lain in this very bed with her and teased: *Feels like I'm out in me Da's old scow when I'm rowing you in me arms, Lisbeth, darlin'.*

Lisbeth squeezed her eyes shut on a surge of grief and pain. It had been a storm like this that brought his father's old scow, the *White Gull*, ashore in pieces on the rocks down past Lobster Cove, and broke Lisbeth's heart with it. Declan had not been aboard and was nowhere to be found, plucked away clean as the jetsam such storms scrubbed from the shore.

A year ago, that had been. Every time Lisbeth awoke with his voice in her ears, she told herself she had to stop hoping. But she couldn't, not quite.

Lightning flashed, sharp and violent, and seared her eyes.

Lisbeth flinched and clutched the blanket. The men of Lobster Cove—old salts and mariners, many of them—had examined the wreckage of the *White Gull* and speculated she'd been hit by lightning while at sea. No man, they said, could have ridden out such a storm.

"Not even a strong swimmer like Declan," Lisbeth said aloud, now.

The words hung in the dark air of the room, burning Lisbeth's heart the way the bright flash seared her eyes. She did not want to believe them.

She must.

Outside the wind rose, threatening a gale, and screamed around the stones of the cottage. Surely that had awakened her. Not his voice.

Lisbeth.

There—she heard it again, a mere whisper of sound riding the tail end of the thunder. Just so had his voice rumbled in her ear when he made love to her, warm and so very Irish.

Suddenly she could lie in the bed no longer. She fought her way free of the blankets and swung her bare feet down to the icy floor. Fumbling, she reached for the candle on the table beside the bed and in her haste knocked it over. She heard it roll away across the planks.

No light, then. She waited for the next flash of lightning to illuminate the tiny room. She had not wed Declan for his wealth or possessions but for the charm he wore like a second skin, and the devilry in his eyes. She had married him because he was all she'd imagined wanting since the age of eleven.

She stumbled to the window and strained to see through the rain that streaked the glass. The next flash showed her the rocks in front of the cottage and the sea heaving itself up like the back of a monster to top them. The storm must be right over her. And remembering—remembering made her tremble.

She recalled the first time she'd seen Declan O'Shea. She, her sister Ellie, and her parents had just moved to Lobster Cove from St. John's, Newfoundland when Lisbeth and Ellie showed up for their first day of school at the one-room schoolhouse on First Street. Ellie, older than Lisbeth and more outgoing, took things such as the first day of school in her stride. Even before they entered the building, she struck up conversations with two girls her age and made friends.

Lisbeth, feeling shy, stood on her own, eyeing the other students—all ten of them. Some looked young enough to be just starting to learn their letters. One girl, near Lisbeth's age, wore a fine frock and button-up shoes, and stood with her nose in the air.

Three lads also appeared to be near Lisbeth's age. One stood as quietly as she, an awkward-looking boy with no meat on his bones, a pinched face, and hair black as coal. The other two had to be brothers, they looked so alike—both with flaming red hair, faces full of freckles, and eyes wild as those of foxes. The brothers fussed and pushed each other until the teacher called them all inside. Then one of them held the door for Lisbeth and gave her a smile that lit the morning—and her heart. Not until the teacher called roll did Lisbeth learn his name: Declan O'Shea.

She believed she had loved him from that very day.

Another flash and again her thoughts flew back in time. It had rained on the day of their wedding—bad luck, some folks said. Lisbeth hadn't cared about the weather because Declan had become hers forevermore.

But the bad luck had followed. Almost a year to the day from her wedding had come the storm, so like this one, that had snatched Declan from her life.

She turned from the window blindly, not wanting another glimpse of the raging sea lest she begin raving at it in return, screaming and demanding what it owed her. She told herself she should bury her head under the bedclothes, burrow there, and pray for morning. How many more of these endless nights could she endure?

Lightning flashed once more, flooding her eyes with brightness. In the doorway of the bedroom stood a figure wearing dripping oilskins, only the matching sou'wester missing from his bare head.

Declan.

In the sudden darkness that followed the lightning, she moaned his name and then shouted it.

"Declan? Declan, Declan!"

She heard movement, the scrape of a boot on the floorboards, the flap of his coat as he turned and left the doorway.

With a sob, she followed. Hands stretched before her like a blind woman, she felt for him, stubbed her bare toe on the leg of the bedstead, and faltered. She blundered from the room in his wake.

The cottage boasted but three rooms: this bedroom they had shared, another smaller bedroom she'd dreamed of someday using as a nursery for her children, and the main room which combined parlor and kitchen. The darkness of the main room enfolded Lisbeth like black velvet. She had but a glimpse of paler darkness as the front door opened and closed again.

"Declan!"

She followed after him, her heart torn between gladness and pain. He was here! But if he truly were here, returned by some miracle from the same sea that had stolen him, why would he go from her?

She reached the door, tore it open, and stared out into the storm. Waves and salt spray poured over the stones in front of the cottage. Static filled the air, and lightning arced overhead, the thunder competing for dominance with the crash of the rain.

Wearing only her nightgown, Lisbeth was immediately soaked to the skin. The wind tore at her hair, and she strained to catch sight of the figure she had glimpsed in the doorway.

From the cottage, as well she knew, a path led either north to a narrow strip of shingle or south toward Lobster Cove. Which way might he have gone? She could see nothing but storm, the raging elements that matched the furor now in her heart. Would he head down to the sea? Most of this coast consisted of sheer rock, but the O'Sheas possessed that stony beach where they had hauled up their boats and readied their lobster traps.

The boats were all gone; the *White Gull* lay in pieces. Why would Declan go there? Having come home to her, why would he leave at all?

She walked barefoot to a break in the rocks where the sea poured in like a gray beast, alive and wild. No one but a madman would be down on that strip of shingle now.

She turned her head toward the track but saw nothing. The thought came to her: *Maybe I imagined it.* But she had heard the scrape of his boots on the floor. She had seen his hair ruffled by the force of the storm.

A dream, then. She'd had them before, yes, but never, never so real. She returned to the cottage, where she shut the door and hurried to the fireplace. With clumsy hands, she searched for matches and the stub of a candle. Her fingers shook so violently it took her three attempts to put flame to the wick.

The light took hold slowly and seemed pitifully inadequate. Thrusting it aloft, Lisbeth retraced her steps to the door of her room, careful to keep the hem of her now-sodden garment swept back, her eyes on the floor.

A trail of wet led its way to the bedroom door and culminated on the threshold.

The very place where he had stood.

The candle tumbled from her suddenly numb fingers, and the flame went out.

Chapter Two

The storm pulled off before dawn and moved away up the coast toward Nova Scotia. Lisbeth, who slept no more that night, dressed herself and, before going outside, mopped up the wet floor by the dim light that seeped over the windowsills.

The wind still blew aloft, raking the sky and stretching the clouds into long streamers. But areas of blue showed between, and far out the sea took on a deep cobalt hue. Inshore, the waves remained tumultuous. They tossed themselves over the break wall, sending an occasional spurt of spray half way up her walk.

She stood wrapped tight in her shawl, her hair flapping and her skirts pressed against her legs. Her gaze plundered the shore the way the storm had. She did not want to admit to herself she looked for signs—for proof—of what she had seen last night, some tangible evidence beyond the water on the floor saying she hadn't dreamed the figure in the doorway. In the hours before dawn she'd been over and over it, and doubt had crept in. She might well have dreamed it.

She must have dreamed it.

Just as she must have dropped that water on the floor herself, shed it before she caught herself, when she came in.

She must have shed it.

Because, desire it as she would, Declan couldn't

come back to her. He lay dead somewhere at the bottom of that wild ocean.

Could the heart produce such an illusion through sheer desire?

Unable to keep still an instant longer, she walked down the path to the shingle, going carefully and marking the items that littered the stones. Such storms as the one last night swept the shore clean of flotsam and deposited new things in exchange: driftwood, broken floats, even a lobster pot lying dashed and broken.

Was it one of Declan's? After he died, the men had hauled in his pots and given her the money from his last catch. This broken cage, then, must represent someone else's misfortune.

The sea clawed at the shingle, slow to calm. Almost at once, Lisbeth's feet became soaked and cold, but she walked on. If he'd come in a skiff, he would have put in here; it was the only place.

Yet she saw no signs on the stones and, anyway, what skiff could weather such a storm?

She turned and walked the other way, back toward the path that led to town. The wind blew her hair into her eyes, and she pawed it out of the way. She had the mad idea she might find his sou'wester lying in a sodden patch of bright yellow where it had blown from his head.

Mad idea.

She passed her cottage, climbed the rise where the path angled up along the cliff toward Lobster Cove, and saw him.

A man walking toward her.

Not the man she sought.

This one had no beacon of flaming red hair declaring his Irish blood. And a dog walked at his side. The man's hair and the dog's coat matched in hue—black, with the deep gleam of a crow's wing. Lisbeth knew him by the dog and his hair, and she tried to deny the way her heart fell.

"Good morning, Rab," she called when he drew near enough. "What brings you way up here so early?"

"Came to make sure you survived that blow last night."

He and the dog kept walking toward her. A big man, and the blacksmith in town, Rab Sinclair could not be called handsome—not as Declan had been.

Handsome as the Devil, am I not? Declan had often joked, with that note of cocky confidence in his voice.

But Rabbie Sinclair had a pleasant face, broad and strong like the rest of him, and that glossy black hair worn over-long, and those deep blue eyes the same color the sea had now turned, far out. Lisbeth wondered again why he had never married; a sheer waste of a good man.

For Rabbie Sinclair was above all else a good man. Lisbeth had known him from that first day at school—the thin, dark boy straight off a ship from Scotland, orphaned and with his keep to earn in the world.

How that pale, scrawny boy had grown!

She turned her attention to the dog, a male Newfoundland. Rab had accepted him in trade three years ago for a job he'd done for some fishermen from off the Grand Banks. The dog had been a mere pup then, a ball of black fur and paws that Lisbeth had helped name. Like the man, the dog had grown magnificently.

The three of them met on the path, and Lisbeth

reached to pat the dog's head. "Good morning, Kelpie." She added, addressing the dog rather than his master, "Surely you did not walk all the way out here from concern for me?"

Rab shrugged his big shoulders. He wore a fisherman's sweater nearly the same color as his eyes, and Lisbeth wondered which of the townswomen had knitted it for him. Several of them pursued Rab the way they had pursued Declan before Lisbeth married him.

"Friends look out for one another," he said. The deep burr of Scotland still colored his voice after more than a decade in Maine. "Besides, Kelpie here is always eager for a walk."

Lisbeth felt his gaze touch her face in swift inspection. "Are you well, Lisbeth?"

Not wanting to lie to him outright, Lisbeth merely nodded. Rabbie, a good friend indeed, checked on her often, seeming to take the mile-long trek from Lobster Cove in stride.

She knew decency should prompt her to invite him in for a cup of tea, but the cottage stood dark and cold. Besides, she wanted to be alone to search the path for a crumpled sou'wester, for signs her dream might prove true.

The wind seized the end of her shawl and pulled it from her shoulders. Rab reached out quickly enough to keep it from soaring away.

"Mad to stand out here in the cold," he observed. "You'll catch your death."

Lisbeth looked up and encountered his gaze. The blue eyes, trapped between black lashes, narrowed at her, and she tried to decide what she saw there: concern, surely, and the kindness Rab wore like a second skin.

He had once told her a lad cut adrift from his home at the age of fourteen—orphaned and landless, sent to a new life—learned many things quick and hard. Especially how it felt to be in need, how terrifying the world could be, and the value of kindness.

Lucky Kelpie, she thought, who had landed in his hands. And fortunate the woman who eventually won his heart.

She sighed deeply, surrendering at last the compulsion to search for what might not exist.

"Will you come in for some breakfast?"

"I will not say 'no.' "

She turned, and they walked together, back the way she had come, to the cottage. She'd left in such haste the door still stood open, driven back and forth by the wind.

What would Rab make of that? He frequently voiced the opinion that with Declan gone Lisbeth should not stay here alone.

"Any damage in town?" she asked, for something to say, as they pushed into the dim front room.

"Aye." Rabbie closed the door carefully and stood looking about. With the large dog, he seemed to overfill the room the way Declan never had.

But then, Declan was quicksilver, light and ever-moving. Rabbie was the granite of those rocks on the shore.

"That big loblolly pine—you know, the one at the head of Main Street—got hit by lightning. Came down and blocked the road."

Lisbeth, striving desperately for a natural reaction, fixed her features into an expression of shocked surprise. "Anyone hurt?"

"No one living and breathing, but plenty of

property damage. Lisbeth, 'tis cold in here. Why have you let the fire go out?"

"I—" Lisbeth stared at him helplessly.

"Never mind, let me."

An expert with fire was Rab, after tending the blaze in the forge so many years. Lisbeth knew he thought it a sin to let a fire die.

Now she removed her shawl and watched as Kelpie lay down with a grunt and Rab bent over the cold hearth, his hair sliding over his forehead like black silk.

As he worked to kindle a fire, he stole little looks about the room; Lisbeth wondered what he saw. True, the place felt bleak to her, but she blamed that on Declan's absence. Her life felt bleak, withal. She supposed she had not been keeping up with things as she should. She couldn't remember the last time she'd swept the floor or shaken out the rugs. Her work lay in a pile on the wooden bench by the window—for she earned her keep as a seamstress—but little enough other color enlivened the place. It felt not only cold but uninhabited, and none of the lamps had been trimmed.

When he had the fire going to his satisfaction, Rab straightened from the hearth and looked Lisbeth in the eyes.

"Tell me, Lisbeth, when are you going to put your grief behind you and take up your life?"

Chapter Three

The interior of Lisbeth O'Shea's cottage felt like death: Rab couldn't describe it any other way. The cold that filled it went beyond the physical and struck at his soul.

He supposed that must be the fey Highlander in him talking. More than ten years out of Scotland and he had not succeeded in leaving it behind. He remembered his grandmother telling him, before his world fell apart and he was forced to leave home, "We are knowing things in our blood, lad. Never question that sense. You come by it honestly."

Rab knew now that the woman standing before him had been honed to her marrow. He would give all he had to help her, but he did not know how. He might offer friendship and comfort; he had already given her his heart.

How frail and broken she looked, stranded in this devastated place with the reflection of sorrow in her eyes! Why did he love her so completely and so helplessly? He could not say; he simply had ever since the moment he first saw her, back at the Lobster Cove schoolhouse all those years ago. Since then she had grown into a woman he could only admire—hardworking, generous and kind, giving him no reason to change his feelings.

Of course he hadn't understood what he felt for her back then. He merely knew how much he enjoyed watching the lass who sat across the aisle and one row up from him, catching the curve of her cheek when she turned her head, counting the curls on her shoulders.

Her hair had been golden then, a child's hair still. Now it had darkened to the ashen hue belonging to a woman, but still streaked with gold from the sun. She never failed to look beautiful to him, with her delicate features and those eyes that made him think of magical things: highland mist and the color of the sea loch back home on a cloudy day.

At school she had been a comfort to him, a balm to a lad aching from the loss of everything he loved, thrown onto this rocky shore with an impossible way to make—a new master, kind but firm, and the sheer hard work of the forge. He had pinned all his dreams on Lisbeth Parsons.

She, of course, had never seen anyone but Declan O'Shea.

And the true tragedy of it, she had never once seen Declan for what he truly was.

She would not now. Declan was dead, a martyr to the sea, a memory. Lisbeth cherished him yet.

He remembered all too well the day Declan had drowned. A storm like the one just past it had been. And that had brought him out here early today, concern for Lisbeth foremost in his mind. What might the Widow O'Shea do here alone when despair overtook her?

He gazed at her now, unable to hide his concern. She'd dropped weight since Declan's death. Her fingers, which she twisted in her skirt, looked like little more than sticks.

Gently he asked, "When are you going to move into town? 'Tis not right, you out here on your own."

She shook her head and made no reply.

"There's that room at Mrs. Taylor's," he pressed. "She's still looking to let it."

"I don't want to live with Mrs. Taylor. She's a terrible gossip."

Rab knew it for truth. "But in town you'd be nearer your clients. And near your friends."

He, himself, lived in back of Howard's Blacksmith Shop on Maple Street—his now, since the death of his patron, Tip Howard, three years ago. On his deathbed Tip had told Rab he'd become more son to him than apprentice, and earned the inheritance.

"Frannie's there," he went on. Frannie Becker, Lisbeth's closest friend, was as worried about her as he.

"Frannie has two small children and her own life to live," Lisbeth replied.

"That changes nothing. Here, sit down before you fall."

Impulsively he towed her to a stool and sat her down. Then he hoisted the kettle—bone dry—and shook his head. "Have you tea in the house?"

"Some."

He snatched up a bucket for the well. Kelpie gave him a look from soulful eyes in passing.

Guard, he told the dog in his mind. The two of them did not always need words to communicate.

The wind tore at him when he went out, just like his emotions. He wanted so badly to gather Lisbeth up in his arms and carry her back to Lobster Cove— not to Mrs. Taylor's but to his quarters, warm and safe behind the shop. He longed to confess all his feelings for her, a thing he'd never done. Declan O'Shea had always stood in the way.

Rab smiled bitterly as he filled the wooden bucket. *As he did still.*

Inside, Lisbeth remained where he'd put her, which further discomfited him. For all her apparent fragility, he knew her to have a stubborn, independent streak. If that had been beaten down, she must be in even worse straits than he thought. He poured water into the kettle and swung it over the fire.

"Winter will be coming in a few months." He resumed the conversation as if it had never been interrupted. "Say you'll be away out of this place before then."

"I will think on it, Rab."

"Do you promise me?"

She nodded.

Of course, he told himself sadly, *thinking on* wasn't the same as *moving on.*

"How are you fixed for firewood?" he asked, eyeing the meager supply beside the hearth.

"I mean to gather some driftwood once the wind dies."

He turned his attention to the shelves that flanked the fireplace. "And have you enough foodstuffs? Your cupboards look unco' bare."

"I mean to go into town tomorrow and purchase a few things."

"Write me out a list; I'll bring what you want."

She stared at him. In the radiance cast by the newly-kindled fire, he saw her eyes fill with tears. "I have no money to pay, Rab. I will soon; I'm finishing a job for Mignon La Marche, and she pays well. But right now…"

"Do not worry about the coin. I will be able to get you credit at the mercantile. Have you flour?

Butter? Lamp oil?"

Stonily she said, "Mr. Beatty will not give me any more credit. I have not been able to pay much on the last bill. I gave him what I could, but you see, Declan owed him quite a bit when he—"

She could not speak the word: *died*. Rab wanted to say it for her, make her face it, accept that she might resume the life she appeared to have abandoned when the damned pieces of the *White Gull* washed ashore.

But he dared not.

Very gently he told her, "I will sort it."

Kelpie, perhaps sensing Lisbeth's emotions, got up and thrust his great head onto her lap. Her hands came up and caressed the dog, buried themselves in his thick, black fur, and Rab saw her ease for the first time.

"Would you like me to leave Kelpie here with you for company?" he offered.

Again her fey, shadowed eyes flew to his. "He would be miserable away from you. You know how he likes to keep you in sight."

True, Kelpie had become a feature of the blacksmith's, always lying at the door and rarely letting Rab move far without him.

"But he loves you," Rab told Lisbeth. *I love you.* He ached to add those words.

The water in the kettle began to sing. Rab searched out two mugs and a small measure of tea, located a stub of a loaf and morsel of butter. He brewed the first, toasted the second, and presented it all to her wordlessly.

"You are far too good to me, Rab Sinclair."

He said nothing as he watched her sip from the mug and nibble at the crust without appetite. Kelpie rested his chin on her knee.

"You've not been eating," Rab observed at last, "nor looking after yourself. What would Declan say?" He delivered the last words with deliberation as he might those of a holy incantation. He himself had detested Declan O'Shea to his very roots. But if anything could make Lisbeth care, it was the thought of him.

To his surprise she laughed unsteadily. "I am not sure he would notice. Always wrapped up in his own business was Declan."

Wrapped up in himself, more like, Rab thought sourly. He had rarely met a man whose life centered more on his own needs and wants. And he did very little real business of any kind. True, he put out in the old boat he'd inherited from his father, and duly came in again, hauled a few lobster pots while he was out on the sea. But the man had been lazy to the bone, used to getting by on his charm, which he possessed in spades.

Why couldn't Lisbeth see any of that? She never had, though, and regarded her husband still as some kind of minor Irish god.

Lisbeth had worked as a seamstress even while Declan lived, helping to keep the household. She had done what she could to maintain the cottage, just like Declan's mother before her. The O'Shea men of this shore, father and sons alike, had been feckless.

Both Declan's parents had predeceased him, his mother from overwork and his father in a drunken fall. His brother Pat had left Lobster Cove right after the pieces of the *White Gull* washed ashore. He hadn't been out with Declan that fateful day, too smart to take the boat to sea with a blow coming, and had been safe in the tavern with friends.

"He would not want you pining away here, still," Rab told Lisbeth, not sure but it was a lie. Who knew what had motivated Declan besides his own welfare? He had loved holding people in thrall to him, especially women. Indeed, before these two wed he'd been chased by many a lass, including the Mignon Lisbeth had just mentioned, who now owned the big house up on the bluff.

Mignon—also used to getting what she wanted—had chased Declan mercilessly. Rab had prayed Declan would choose her, but in the end he had chosen this pale slip of a lass with the wide eyes, spill of fair hair, and—back then—merry laugh.

That didn't mean he had been faithful to her.

Rab closed his eyes for a moment, fighting the desire to tell Lisbeth all he knew, destroy this vision she cherished of her dead husband, free her from the past to—he hoped—love again. He couldn't. He feared it would destroy not only Lisbeth's opinion of her husband but her spirit.

"Come back to town wi' me," he beseeched, speaking from his heart. "Do not make me leave you here alone."

"That's just it." She set her mug aside, leaned forward, and touched Rab's hand. He felt the imprint of her fingers all the way up his arm, to his heart. "I am not alone," she confided, "for I saw Declan last night."

Chapter Four

"I am worried about Lisbeth," Rab announced. He stood in the doorway of Frannie Becker's kitchen, feeling far too large for the cramped space. Mad confusion reigned: Frannie had two bairns under the age of two, the newest a babe of barely six months, now held in her arms. The toddler, a robust lad, ran rather than walked everywhere and seemed particularly vocal with his demands.

Frannie shot Rab a look. "Close the door for pity's sake, before Eddie escapes again. I've no desire to chase him down the street another time."

Rab eased the door shut behind his considerable bulk, trying to occupy as little space as possible. "You have your hands full there, and no mistake," he observed. Maybe Lisbeth was right; Frannie had no room and likely little energy to spare. "Where's Ed?"

"At work. He went in early; we need the coin."

Ed Becker worked at Sawyer's lumber yard all the hours God sent, to keep his little family.

Frannie shifted the bairn—a daughter—in her arms. "I'm worried about Lisbeth as well, Rab. She's stopped coming to church. And she used to walk in sometimes to see me. The Lord knows I was in no condition to walk out there when I was carrying this little one." She jostled the child. "Worse than that, she seems to have lost her spark and that strength she always had about her, beneath all the softness. I'd go see her, but…"

"Aye, I see."

Wee Eddie began climbing the back of a chair, which wobbled beneath him. Rab snatched the lad up in his arms. Eddie, sticky all over his face with what looked like jam, smiled at him.

"I also see this fellow's had his breakfast."

"Would you like a cup of tea?"

"Just had one." He thought of the gloomy cottage he'd left, and the woman in it. "I walked out to see Lisbeth this morning."

"How did she come through the storm?"

Rab shook his head. "I saw no damage. But you're right, Frannie. She's not the lass she was, nor right in herself, in her mind."

"In her mind?" Frannie echoed. She stared at Rab, her eyes the same exact size and shape as Eddie's—deep brown. "I know she's still in mourning—it's only been a year—but though it's taken the heart out of her I did not think it had turned her mind." Frannie lowered her voice. "You know how she loved him."

"Aye." Rab felt sick inside. Frannie, no fool, had a good idea what Declan's true character had been. But Rab had managed to hide from her his true feelings about Lisbeth.

He drew a deep breath and set Eddie down carefully. "She says she saw him—*Declan*—last night."

"What!" Frannie's mouth fell open, and for an instant Rab thought she'd drop the child in her arms. He could see her thoughts move in her wide eyes. "Well, she must have dreamed it. That storm will have brought things back."

"That's what I thought. But she was insistent. Says there was water all over the floor where he stood in the doorway of their room."

"Sweet mercy! Did you see the water?"

"She had already mopped it up."

"It will be her imagination, poor lamb."

"Aye, but I tell you it went hard with me, leaving her out there alone, Fran. She's not looking after herself—almost no food on her shelves, and the place was cold. I collected some driftwood before I came away, and I mean to take her a load of things from Beatty's."

"You're a good friend, Rab Sinclair."

"Not good enough, letting her get in that state."

"What can I do to help?"

"I was hoping you'd persuade her to move into Lobster Cove. I did my best to convince her; she would no' listen."

"I'd go and talk to her, gladly, but—" Frannie gestured helplessly, encompassing the room and the children. "I'll try and make it out there in the next few days—I can ask Ed's mother to look after these two for a few hours. I'll take Lisbeth one of my seed cakes. She used to love them."

"I would appreciate it. She may listen to you better than me."

"I hope so."

"I offered to leave Kelpie there with her, the place seemed so lonely. She would no' hear of it."

"A shame she and Declan never had a child, something of him she might keep." Fran sighed. "Anyway, you'd make a strange sight without Kelpie at your side. Where is he now?"

"Just outside the door," Rab admitted. "Frannie, when you go to visit, try and persuade her away out of that place for the winter."

"I promise to do my best. Now you had better get

off. You've a forge to run."

"Aye, and half a dozen jobs waiting."

Yet he hesitated. "You do no' suppose grief truly has unsettled her mind?"

Frannie looked concerned. "If it has you this worried, I'll go out and see her tomorrow. I'll let you know what I think then."

"Aye," he murmured, but he went away little comforted.

****

Beating on glowing iron and sweating over the forge usually brought Rab a measure of peace, but not today. Stripped down to his trousers, protected by only a leather apron, he enjoyed exercising muscles built over time and using skill combined with intention to accomplish a job. Hot iron might be mutable; fire was not. A living substance, it required accommodation, tending, and consideration if it were to cooperate with him. Over the past years at work in this place, he and fire had come to terms. He respected it and it consented to do his bidding—most of the time.

Tip Howard, who had liked to talk while he worked and especially liked to talk to the young Scots lad who remained mostly silent, used to say that in ancient times blacksmiths were considered wizards, wreakers of magic. They controlled the fire and caused iron to obey them. Not many men could survive the forge, a truth Rab learned in the most personal way as he grew. It took a certain kind of man.

"Either the fire chooses you or it doesn't," Tip told him at the beginning. "Let's see, lad, if it will heed you."

It had, but persuading it required an enormous

119

amount of work, sweat, and more singed skin than Rab could measure. He knew, now, the fire took its price.

As did the sea, he supposed.

In the old days, the magician smiths had wrought swords and other weapons that, if strong enough, brought victory in battle. Now Rab made plows and other farm implements, horse shoes, and fancy fenders for women's hearths.

He tossed the black hair out of his eyes and wiped his perspiring forehead with an equally sweaty forearm. Today the work brought him very little contentment. He couldn't keep his thoughts from the cottage up the shore.

Aye, well, he would finish up a few jobs, go to Beatty's, and see could he run some things back out there before the light died.

He pumped up the fire and began making a list in his mind: she would need flour, lard, eggs, some dried peas, and butter if he could get it. Vegetables would be fine if Beatty had any—carrots and potatoes. And he should take something to tempt Lisbeth's appetite, just in case Frannie did not make it out there with the seed cake. But what?

Upon the thought, he heard Kelpie's tail thump. The dog lay just outside the door in the pale sunshine; a wag was his usual greeting to visitors.

Rab looked up and saw a woman enter. Women usually sent their men to the forge; this woman, though, had never married.

The teacher at the schoolhouse, Emily Cooper must be a year or two older than Rab. Plain to look at, she had a lively, intelligent mind and a droll sense of humor Rab enjoyed. Lately she had made any excuse possible to come to the shop, bringing broken implements for the school and her home. He had just completed the latest, a handle for the classroom woodstove.

"Never say it has grown so late," he greeted her. "School over already?"

"I just dismissed the children."

Ah, and he would need to get to Beatty's and up the shore before it got much later.

"I have your handle all ready." He swung away, picked up the piece from the bench, and turned back to catch Miss Cooper staring at his nether regions.

Not used to women looking at him that way, he felt a stab of surprise at the speculation in her eyes.

Miss Cooper, apparently not a bit discomfited, smiled at him. "I can always rely on you, Mr. Sinclair, to take care of my little projects." She swung her purse up by its strings. "What do I owe you?"

"Only our agreed price."

She came closer, and he considered her; tall and slender, she wore her soft, brown hair in a loose bun at the nape of her neck. She might be a fine woman, but she was no Lisbeth.

She placed the coin in his palm, being sure to let her fingers linger. "Thank you. You do such fine work. I keep saying I should bring the children down here one nice afternoon, let the lads see a man's work."

Rab mopped his forehead again, but not from the heat this time. "That's an interesting idea."

"Will you be taking an apprentice?"

"I hadn't thought on it." He'd hoped for a son of his own, but that did not look likely in the near future.

"I have a student—Dougie Grier. You know

him?"

"Sure."

"Born on the wrong side of the blanket, you understand. Just like his younger brother."

Rab blinked. Most woman of his acquaintance didn't speak of such things. Dougie's mother, Maggie, worked selling ale at the Hogshead and occasionally, so it was rumored, sold or gave away her favors, as well. He'd heard her sons had two different fathers.

"Dougie's a good lad," Miss Cooper went on, "big for his age. He struggles with his letters and numbers, but he listens and tries hard. I think he'd do better with his hands than his head."

"This job takes both." Rab shrugged. "But send him round. Not today—I have an errand to run."

"I will. You're a good man, Rab Sinclair."

"I was given a chance at his age." And he'd always been grateful. "Why can't I offer the same?"

"His mother's no better than she should be, but at least she's sent him to school. And we can't hold her behavior against him."

"Certainly not. If I do decide to take him on, I would want him to keep attending school, as well." That was something upon which Tip had insisted, for him.

"Just because you earn your living by your brawn doesn't mean you have to be an ignoramus, lad," he'd said in his understated Yankee way. "Get your letters and your sums, so you'll know when a man's trying to cheat you. Learn to read books, and you'll never pass a lonely night."

That last was a lie: Rab had spent a boatload of lonely nights with a book in his hands.

Miss Cooper nodded as if satisfied and turned

away to the door. At the last minute she looked back. "Will you be attending the autumn dance, Mr. Sinclair?"

He made a rueful gesture. "Can you see me dancing?"

"As a matter of fact, I can." To his increased shock, she winked at him before she went out the door and left him staring.

A word about the author...

Born and raised in Western New York, Laura Strickland has been an avid reader and writer since childhood. Her interests include history—particularly Celtic lore and legend—and animal welfare. Although she loves to travel to the settings of her various books, she can usually be found at home not far from Lake Ontario with her husband and her "fur" child, a rescue dog.